CROWN ME!

BY

Kathryn Lay

Holiday House / New York

3   5   7   9   10   8   6   4   2

Library of Congress Cataloging-in-Publication Data
Lay, Kathryn.
Crown me! / by Kathryn Lay.—1st ed.
p. cm.
Summary: As part of an experiment in a social studies class,
fifth graders Justin Davies and Andrea Carey are declared
king and queen for two weeks, but they soon learn that royal life
is a royal pain as their classmates revolt.
ISBN 0-8234-1845-6 (hardcover)
(1. School—Fiction. 2. Kings, queens, rulers, etc.—Fiction.
3. Friendship—Fiction. 4. Leadership—Fiction.) I.Title.

PZ7.L445Cr 2004
(Fic)—dc22   2004040607

ISBN-13: 978-0-8234-1845-9 (hardcover)

For my agent, Erin Murphy,
and my editors Mary Cash and Suzanne Reinoehl
who believed in and helped shape this book.

For Richard,
my knight in shining armor,
and Michelle, my forever princess,
for their love, encouragement and support.

For my amazing court jesters:
Melissa Russell, Diane Roberts, Chris Ford,
Jan Peck, Gerelle Woods, David R. Davis, BJ Stone, Sue
Ward, Trish Holland, Tom McDermott, Janet Fick,
Deborah J. Lightfoot, Debra Deur,
and Amanda Jenkins, who keeps me sane
and laughing every Tuesday.

To my royal advisors:
Brett, Tammy, Jonathan, Aaron, and Stephen,
who've always been there.

And for my parents,
Gladys and Bobby Petrey,
who believed.

Contents

Chapter 1

♕

Equal Rights for Boys, Too

Future Politician's Rule #1—
Never get caught.

There is a time in every kid's life when he has to stand up for something important. This was my time. If I was going to be president of the United States someday, I had to start at the bottom. And for me, the bottom was Payton Intermediate School.

I had set my first political goal at Payton. A goal that every kid in school would thank me for. They just didn't know it yet. I, Justin Davies, was going to be the next president of the fifth-grade student council. We were the Payton Penguins, and I planned to be the head penguin.

I had lots of ideas to gain their votes, and I

was about to put my first plan into action. I crept along the corridor outside the boys' gym, then stopped to peer down the empty hall. I turned toward my two best friends and put a finger to my lips.

We were almost there. It had been amazingly easy so far. Coach Friedman had been busy calming down Willie Fisher when Carlos, Lester, and I slipped out of the gym. You could always count on Willie to fall during gymnastics, a perfect diversion when an escape plan was needed.

"This time, you've gone too far," Carlos whispered, dribbling an imaginary basketball. He danced around me and did a jump shot over my head.

"Stop that," I said. "Someone will hear your squeaky shoes."

I couldn't believe he was going to chicken out on me already. "Look, I thought you guys were with me on this! The girls got the new gym equipment just because Priscilla's rich parents donated the money. It's not fair, and as future president of the United States and of the fifth-grade student council, I plan to make sure everyone gets a fair shake."

I let out a breath. I hadn't meant to give a long speech, but I just couldn't help it. Carlos and Lester clapped their hands against their ears and moaned.

"Did you guys see the mess in front of the

2

school today?" Lester asked. "Looked like a forest threw up."

Carlos laughed. "Good one. Wonder what happened?"

"Be quiet," I ordered. Sheesh, a few torn-up bushes outside the school weren't important right now. With Carlos's basketball obsession and Lester always making a joke out of everything, I wondered if it had been a mistake to let them come with me.

When we reached the door to the girls' gym, I marched inside, waving in that special presidential way I'd been practicing.

"Eek!" Priscilla Ashworth-Cole screamed. "Boys!"

"Out!" Mrs. Hawk shouted, walking toward us.

I cleared my throat. "Mrs. Hawk, I'm sure you've heard of the many cases where girls have been allowed in boys' clubs *and* on boys' teams in sports. We are just exercising *our* rights of equality to be a part of the girls' physical education classes. We can alternate on the new gym equipment every day until the boys' gym is equally equipped. . . ."

Mrs. Hawk stared at me a moment, then shook her head. "I heard all about your disruptions and political yip-yap when you were at Donna Park Elementary, Justin."

She nodded at the watching girls. "Continue with your routines."

Andrea Carey stomped across the gym. She stood in front of me and folded her arms. "If I was the teacher I'd give you detention and a bad grade and announce to the whole fifth grade over the loudspeaker that you barged into the girls' gym. If I ran this school, you three would be in detention every day. If I were in charge around here . . ."

I grinned at Carlos and Lester. "Yeah? Good thing you aren't in charge. . . ."

Mrs. Hawk waved Andrea away. She pointed at me. Not at Carlos or Lester. Just at me. "She's not in charge here, but I am. Mrs. Winthrop is used to seeing you in her office by now, and I don't intend to make you a hero. Instead, I'm taking you back to Coach Friedman." Then she turned to Carlos and Lester. "All of you."

I frowned. Carlos and Lester groaned. Getting a lecture from Dragon Lady Winthrop, the principal, would have been much easier. I'd rather eat a dirty gym sock than face Coach Friedman.

"Way to go, Prez," Carlos said, giving me a shove.

"At least we made a statement," I said.

Lester gave me a punch on the arm.

We followed Mrs. Hawk back to the boys' gym. I wondered if the president of the United States felt this way when he got into trouble.

"I see you've found my three deserters."

4

Coach Friedman stomped toward us, rubbing his bald head with his knuckles.

I glanced at Carlos and Lester. It was a bad sign when Coach knuckle-rubbed his head.

Mrs. Hawk nodded. "It seems that our junior lawyer here has decided to make the gym classes coed."

Coach Friedman stared into my eyes. Not many fifth graders were able to meet a teacher eye to eye without looking up. Coach Friedman made up for his short height by having a stare that could melt a kid's braces.

"I'll take care of them," the coach said, giving Mrs. Hawk a smile.

There was a gasp from the other kids, like the ominous hiss of a flat tire. Coach Friedman rarely smiled. It wasn't a pleasant sight.

"But, sir," I began. "As future class president, I feel that—"

Coach snorted and growled. "Ten laps."

"Piece of cake," I mumbled.

"Backward," Coach said with another frightening smile.

After ten backward laps around the gym and lots of teasing by the other guys, we were given late passes from the coach. We changed clothes and raced to history class.

"We're late and it's your fault, Mr. I-Promise-We-Won't-Get-Into-Trouble," Lester said. He punched my arm again.

This time, I punched him back. "You both hate history. I'm the one who's being punished. We've probably already missed Hat Time."

Carlos flung open the door to Mr. Bailey's second-period history class and we burst in like a triple explosion.

"You're tardy, boys," Mr. Bailey said.

I stood beside my desk. My heart drummed against my chest when I saw the crown on Mr. Bailey's head. At least we hadn't missed out on the essay. "Sorry, sir, but our rights were being suppressed by Coach Friedman and Mrs. Hawk. It is because of their desire to control that we find ourselves tardy. Where are our rights? I'll tell you where they are. They—"

Mr. Bailey pointed at my desk. "Sit down. No speeches today. Not yet, at least."

I slid into my chair and turned to grin at Carlos and Lester. They smiled back. I knew they couldn't stay mad for long. We've been friends since second grade. We survived elementary school together and made it to fifth grade. We were supposed to be at the top of the heap. But overcrowding brought changes, and last year a new program began for fifth and sixth graders. The junior high was too crowded for sixth graders, and the elementary school didn't have room for fifth graders. So now we go to Payton Intermediate School. Garner Junior High got the new building, and we got theirs. But no one cares because we also got bigger lockers, and now there are no little kids hanging around us like hyper puppies. For seventh grade we'll go to Garner and *we'll* be the little kids. But thanks to me, we'd made a name for ourselves. Of course, it wasn't a name you say aloud without getting your mouth washed out with soap, but at least we were well known.

"Now that everyone is here, we can begin," Mr. Bailey said.

"Attention, students, I'd like to make an important announcement." Everyone groaned as the principal's voice crackled from the intercom speakers.

"Now what?" Mr. Bailey mumbled. He straightened the crown on his head and leaned against his desk. "Ssh, boys and girls."

"As you've seen and heard by now, the school was vandalized in a most vicious way this past weekend. Our beautiful trees were cut down, flowers uprooted, and shrubs hacked to pieces. If anyone knows *anything* about this, please speak to your teacher or come to the office. Any information will be strictly confidential. Thank you."

Carlos leaned across the aisle and whispered, "I'll bet it was Badger and some of his tough guy friends. If they were on the basketball team, they'd be benched."

Mr. Bailey rapped on his desk with a stapler. "Something you'd like to share with the rest of us, Mr. Mendoza and Mr. Davies?"

I glanced across the room at Badger Crabtree. Badger gnawed on his pencil like a dog chewing a bone. I shook my head. "No, sir."

I wasn't about to accuse Badger out loud. And I wasn't going to be sent from the room on Friday. Especially during Hat Time. Mr. Bailey was the coolest teacher in fifth grade. He had strange ideas to make us learn. Fun ideas. And once every month, we got to study a time period in history that wasn't even in the curriculum yet. We did plays, videos, anything to make history more interesting. The other fifth-grade classes were just finishing up learning about the American Revolution. But we finished last week. Mr. Bailey liked to expand our lessons and we had spent a week on the French Revolution. It was exciting, but Hat Time every week was the best, it was . . .

". . . a special project," Mr. Bailey was saying. "As everyone can see, I'm wearing a crown today. I've borrowed this from the drama department. So, instead of the hat going to the writer of the best essay, I have another surprise for you."

I popped up from my chair. "What! But you've always given the hat to the one with the best essay. You can't change the rules now."

"Justin, sit!" Mr. Bailey ordered. "You are

always complaining about having to follow adult-made rules. I am aware that you have won more hats than anyone, but I have other plans this time." He moved around the room, letting each student look at the crown. "This is just for you to get the feel of the assignment. This time, the reward will be far different, and far more interesting. Keep that in mind as you write. You will have ten minutes to write your essay. Title it 'If I Were King or Queen of Payton Intermediate School I Would . . .' No talking. Don't put your name on the paper. Turn your paper over when you are done."

I stared at my desk. The crown would have been a perfect addition to my collection. I had already won a Civil War general's hat, a Roman helmet, even an old-fashioned mayor's hat. And my favorite, one that looked like something Winston Churchill would have worn.

They were all carefully hung from the rack Dad had made for me. I'd always heard that politicians wore many different hats. Someday I would be the best politician there had ever been. And my first goal was to show everyone in fifth grade what great leader potential I had. Then, when elections for student council came around in three weeks, right after Halloween, they'd beg me to run for office.

A wad of paper landed in my lap. I unfolded it and read the words scribbled in purple ink.

Too bad, Mr. President . . . Not! I'm going to win the essay this time! Andrea.

I stuck my tongue out at her. Not very presidential, but she'd won almost as many hats as I had. And no matter how much I tried to buy them or trade something for them, she wouldn't let me have them, not one. Even the stovepipe President Lincoln hat I wanted so badly.

Well, no way would I let her win this time. If anyone would make a great king, it would be me. If I were king of Payton, everyone would get what they wanted and my leadership would never be forgotten.

I picked up my pen and began writing.

Chapter 2

👑

Crown Me!

Future Politician's Rule #2—
Believe you are a winner,
and you are!

One thing I really liked about Mr. Bailey was how fast he graded tests and read reports. Most teachers took days to let you know if you passed the test that you sweated over, or if the essay you wrote sounded like your dog's ideas. But not Mr. Bailey.

Twenty minutes after we turned in our essays, he told us to close our history books.

"You've all done very well," he said, waving the stack of papers. "In fact, there will be two winners this time."

I looked at Carlos. "Two?"

Carlos shrugged. "I hope it's not me," he whispered back. "I hate reading my essays out loud."

"I wouldn't worry about it," I said. The longest essay Carlos ever turned in was twenty-five words. If it didn't involve basketball, he didn't want to write about it.

Mr. Bailey pointed at us and shook his head before addressing the class. "What have we been studying the past week?"

"Ooh, ooh, I know the answer!" Andrea waved her hand like a flag in a hurricane.

I imagined one day her hand would sail across the room and land in the fish tank.

Mr. Bailey nodded at Andrea.

Andrea stood and looked around as if making sure all eyes were on her. "We've been studying the French Revolution."

"Correct." Mr. Bailey picked up the stack of essays from his desk. "As you've seen from our studies of the American and French Revolutions, monarchy rule isn't always loved by the people. What should a leader be? Is a ruler's power absolute and are those beneath him beyond all hope if the ruler is corrupt?"

We just stared at him. We'd already talked about all these things. I just wanted my prize.

"Before I return your compositions, I'll read the two winners." Mr. Bailey cleared his throat.

"Once I've finished reading your essay, please come stand beside me."

"A crown is worn by a king or queen. In our study of the French Revolution, we've learned that sometimes kings and queens can be cruel. Those aren't the best kind of rulers, because they should always be fair and concerned for the welfare of their people. But then again, peasants are peasants and not always too smart. Or clean. If I were queen, I'd make sure that all the peasants at Payton were required to dress neatly. They'd have to smell good, too. And the girls would have all the best parts in school plays and get to be first in line for lunch and never have to take pop tests, because they're smarter. If I were queen of Payton, the girls would rule and I'd be in charge. We'd have phones in every locker and never have to wear those tacky striped gym shorts again. I would be loved and adored by everyone and never let the peasants cause trouble like in the American and French Revolutions. Mr. Bailey taught us all about these revolutions where the peasants got mad at the royalty, but I think they were just jealous."

Andrea squealed at her best friend, Priscilla, who gave an answering squeal, the kind of sound you only get from girls and dolphins. They squeezed each other's hands before Andrea stood and glided down the aisle. She tossed her dark hair over her shoulder when she passed my desk.

Only Andrea would come up with something as dull as "welfare of their people."

Mr. Bailey held up a sheet of wrinkled and smudged paper. "The next winning essay reads as follows:"

"If I were king of Payton Intermediate School, I'd be the coolest ruler that ever lived. When people said, 'Long live the king,' they'd really mean it. Life would be a blast, if I were king. People would still have to call me 'your highness' and do what I told them, but I'd always be fair to all my voters . . . I mean people. I'd rule the school and, like any good politician, make sure I did EVERYTHING I promised. Ice cream and sodas would flow like water in the cafeteria. We'd have test-free Mondays and Get-Out-of-Homework passes every Friday. If I were King Justin of Payton, there would be a kid's lounge with unlimited video games and pizza. Everyone could trust me, because I wouldn't play favorites (except to my best friends and all the boys). And there would never be broccoli or fish sticks in the cafeteria again!"

I jumped out of my seat. I turned to Carlos and Lester, who whistled and cheered as I raised my clasped hands in a victory salute. I'd seen the mayor do it last year when he'd won.

"Okay, quiet now," Mr. Bailey ordered. "We are going to have a special project, an experiment, a practical demonstration of what we've learned about the French Revolution and rulers. What is true leadership? Corrupt royalty? What is a leader's responsibility to the people? And what about the people's responsibility to their leader? This will be a good project before you consider your next student council votes in a few weeks."

I couldn't help but grin as I swaggered up the aisle to stand beside Andrea. "The French Revolution? Wow, does that mean I get to chop off Andrea's head?"

The classroom erupted in giggles and gasps. Andrea shook her finger at me. "Don't you come near me, you juvenile delinquent."

Mr. Bailey pulled a whistle from his pocket. He put it to his lips and took a deep breath.

Silence filled the room. We knew that if he had to blow the whistle, we would all get extra homework.

"That's better." He slipped the whistle back in its place. "For the next two weeks, Mr. Davies and Miss Garey will be your king and queen. You are their subjects. To make it really interesting, I've chosen the medieval period for our project."

"The what?" Carlos asked.

The medieval period was the most exciting time of all. "Like King Arthur," I shouted. "With knights and dragons and castles."

Mr. Bailey nodded. "King Justin and Queen Andrea will choose two knights to protect and serve them. But first, we'll construct a dungeon. While you are anywhere on the school grounds, you must obey your king and queen. If they feel that you have behaved in a manner unfit toward their royal persons, they may 'throw' you in the dungeon. Meaning, you will move your desk inside and remain there until the project is over or they agree to free you."

I snickered. Everyone else groaned.

Mr. Bailey added, "Obey them as if they were your leaders, that is, unless it is dangerous or illegal. I will be the final judge of anything they ask you to do. If there are disagreements, your king and queen will explain their decisions in front of the whole class. They can decide on their own to throw you into the dungeon, but they must agree together to set you free." He snapped his fingers. "Oh yes, and to keep this in perspective, you will bow or curtsy whenever they pass."

I'd never seen so many shocked faces. Mouths opened. Eyes widened.

I couldn't believe my ears. It was a dream come true. I looked at Andrea. Well, even the best of dreams had its nightmarish parts. But I was king. And the twenty-two kids in front of me were my subjects.

A smile flickered across Mr. Bailey's lips. It was a weird smile, like when Dad told me to "just try the squid, it tastes like chicken."

Mr. Bailey waved toward Andrea and me. "Behold your king and queen. At the end of the two weeks, or if the project should end sooner . . . for any reason . . . we'll talk about what we've learned. I'll also expect a thorough, two-page report about how you felt as king, queen, peasant, or whatever role you end up playing. Now, let's make this room look like a castle."

We spent the rest of class time constructing a dungeon in the back of the room. We borrowed a rollaway partition from the drama department and set it up near the back to separate it from the rest of the class. Everyone would still be able to see Mr. Bailey, of course, and we could see them, but they would officially be in the dungeon. Mr. Bailey hung a sign from the ceiling that read DUNGEON in big red letters.

I could already think of a few of my classmates who I'd love to see in the dungeon.

"How do you curtsy?" Dena Robinson asked.

"Like this," Andrea said, demonstrating for the class.

The boys laughed and began curtsying to one another. Soon, the whole class was practicing their bows and curtsys . . . to everyone except Andrea and me.

When the bell rang for lunch, we grabbed our books and headed for the door.

"Hold on," Mr. Bailey said. "One last thing before you leave. Your new rulers must choose their two knights. Let me know who they are before the end of the school day—preferably now."

Knights? This project was getting cooler all the time.

"No problem," I said. "I choose Carlos Mendoza and Lester Langford."

My friends bowed to each other, then to me. "Thank you, Your Majesty."

"Hey, I get to have a knight, too," Andrea said.

Mr. Bailey nodded. "As I explained, you will have two knights. That's two total, not two each. I'm sorry, Justin, you'll have to choose either Carlos or Lester."

Andrea smiled. "And I choose Priscilla."

I looked from Carlos to Lester and back to Carlos.

Lester pointed to Priscilla. "Girls can't be knights."

"Girls can be anything they want." Andrea winked at Priscilla.

Mr. Bailey shrugged. "Sorry, boys. Fair is fair."

Carlos took a step closer toward me. "Well? Who's going to be your knight?"

Lester moved between us. "Yeah, who?"

When I saw the expressions on their faces, I knew I was in trouble. Big trouble.

Chapter 3

♕

There's Going to Be Trouble Two-Knight

Future Politician's Rule #3—Think before you speak.

I looked at my friends and saw disaster coming, worse than a face full of pimples. I just couldn't choose one over the other.

Carlos and I beat each other up the first day of second grade. Once we were done, we knew that we liked each other. Now we were like peanut butter and jelly, not bad on our own, but great as a team.

Lester got in on the friendship in third grade. When a frog hopped out of Andrea's lunch box one Friday afternoon, Lester took the rap, even though he had walked in on Carlos and me stuffing the frog inside the lunch box. We were a threesome from then on.

"C'mon, Davies, some of us would like to eat lunch before the cafeteria slop turns back into dog food," Badger Crabtree growled from the back of the room.

My eyes focused on Badger's raised fist. I wasn't about to provoke the part-kid, part-rhinoceros now.

"Umm, umm . . ." I looked from Lester to Carlos.

Behind them, someone jumped up and down, waving his arms and grinning at me.

"Choose," Andrea ordered.

"Psst. Psst, over here, Your Majesty," the jumping kid shouted.

"Willie Fisher!" I blurted. Willie? Why had *that* name popped out?

"What!" Carlos and Lester shouted in unison.

Lester grinned. "Oh yeah, real funny, Justin."

I glanced at Carlos. Carlos wasn't smiling.

"Fine," Mr. Bailey said, scribbling a note in a pocket notebook. "The two knights will be Priscilla and Willie."

"But . . . it was a mistake. I didn't mean to say it."

Mr. Bailey said, "Get to lunch everyone." He walked away, leaving me with a knight-mare and two unhappy peasants.

"Let's get out of here," Carlos muttered. "There's a rotten smell in this castle. And this time, it's not your gym shorts, Lester."

My friends walked away. Lester looked back, surprise and hurt on his face.

I opened my mouth but I couldn't think of anything to say.

I wondered if the president of the United States ever hurt his friends' feelings. Had he ever had to choose between his two best friends for a job? It wasn't fair. Politicians had lots of hard decisions to make. I held my head high in what I hoped was a kingly pose.

"It was very smart of you to choose me, Your Majesty," a nasal voice said. "I have a very high IQ and, though not as much as you, a knowledge and love for the political world, too."

I turned to stare at Willie. "Huh?"

"I'm not good at being in charge," Willie continued. "And I can't do any hard work; I'm not very strong. But, if I'd known you wanted me to be your best friend, I'd have sat by you at lunch."

"Best friend?"

Willie squinted up into my face. "Does Your Majesty have a hearing defect? You could borrow my grandpa's hearing aid. He died and doesn't need it anymore. Hey, you can come to my house after school so we could talk about how to run the kingdom. My bike is broken, so we'd have to walk, and my room is a mess, and my mother doesn't like company eating up our food, but . . ." He took a deep breath and frowned as if he'd forgotten what he meant to say.

I folded my arms and studied my knight. Willie was a piece of clay I could mold. Why waste time with someone who wanted to challenge my every decision anyway? Maybe Willie was a perfect knight after all.

"Can't come today. I need to do some kingly thinking on my own this afternoon," I explained. "I better get to lunch. The guys are probably wondering where I am."

Willie followed, running in quick steps to keep up with me. "As your knight, I must insist on staying with you to protect you, Your Majesty."

I was stuck with Willie. "Okay, but give me some room. Don't crowd me."

As we hurried down the hall, Willie kept talking. "I know you want to be student council president. This is a once-in-a-lifetime opportunity for both of us."

"For what?" I asked, wondering how to turn him off.

Willie waved his arms around, hitting me in the head twice. "To better the school. It's always been a dream of mine to help someone like you. Someone who has the power, the popularity, the people's ear. We could be a team."

I shook my head. "Share the presidency? No way."

"Oh no, you'd be president. But I could be your adviser."

I stopped outside the cafeteria doors. "Look, Willie, I don't know why I chose you. It just came out. Carlos and Lester are going to help me win the election. You are going to help me get a good grade. Okay?"

Willie frowned. He shrugged. "Sure, just thought you might like to hear some of my ideas."

I didn't. I had ideas of my own. And my first act as king was to declare a truce with my best friends.

I burst into the cafeteria and crossed the room to where Carlos and Lester were sitting. I swung one leg over the seat to straddle it like a king's mighty steed. It wasn't easy, since the seat was small, round, and attached to the table.

No one was required to sit with their class at lunch, yet everyone in Mr. Bailey's history class had always sat at the same table in their own little groups.

"Boy, I'm starved. What have you guys got worth trading?"

Carlos and Lester stared at me. Carlos said, "Pardon us, King Stab-In-The-Back, but we are only unworthy peasants and must ask you to remove your royalness to another place."

"Aw, come on, guys, *one* of you would've been mad no matter who I chose," I said.

"So now we're both mad," Lester said. "You're just a traitor."

Willie sniffed and said in a shrill voice, "How dare you insult your king!"

"Oh, cool it," Carlos said. "You're still Willie the Whiner, no matter what Mr. Bailey or our mighty king says."

"I am the favored knight of his royal majesty, King Justin of Baileyland . . ." Willie said, his voice shaking.

Lester jabbed Carlos's arm. "Yeah, knight of the living dead."

"Hey, Justin, over here."

I looked up to where Andrea was waving her arms from the front of the long table.

"What?" I yelled.

Mr. Bailey walked up to the table, balancing his lunch tray on a stack of books. "Ssh," he ordered. "This is the school cafeteria, not your backyard. I'm giving up my lunch in the teacher's lounge to monitor this project, and though I'm merely here to observe, I'm still in charge."

Andrea clapped her hands. "Bravo, Mr. Bailey. As you can already see, Justin's idea of leadership will be loud and obnoxious. I, on the other hand, will be an orderly queen. Just imagine what a crude fifth grade we'd have if Justin was the ruler? But the school would be filled with respect, beauty, and comfort if I was in charge."

I grinned when Mr. Bailey rolled his eyes. At least he was on to Andrea.

"Hey, didn't there used to be someone else sitting with us at lunch?" Carlos asked.

Lester chewed the hot dog he'd stuffed in his mouth and glanced my way. "Yeah, some guy who said he was our friend. Guess he left town."

I gave my *friends* one last look before slipping off the chair. "Fine, peasants, enjoy your stupid lunch."

I turned and almost tripped over Willie. "Your royal king needs space," I barked at my knight, then walked over to Andrea. "Well, O Queen-Of-Kiss-Up, what do you want?"

"We have to sit at the head of *our* table," Andrea said, pointing to the two empty seats beside her and Priscilla. "We're the queen and king and can't mix with the common people at mealtime."

"Sure," I said. I'd show everyone that I was a great choice for king and even better for student council president. I sat in the chair farthest from the girls. Willie belched, wiped his mouth on his sleeve, and plopped down beside Priscilla, who wrinkled her nose and scooted closer to Andrea.

I ate my lunch and watched my friends. They huddled together at the other end of the table, whispering.

"So, are you enjoying yourself?" Mr. Bailey asked, chewing his lip as if to hide a smile. "Is ruling a monarchy government all you thought it would be?"

"No problem," I said. I stuffed the rest of my sandwich in my mouth, then picked up my milk carton and held it in the air. "Hey, peasants, pay attention, please!" I sputtered.

Everyone at the table stopped talking and looked at me. I stood and said, "Long live King Justin. The next two weeks are going to be the best. I hereby promise to rule Mr. Bailey's fifth-grade history class with fairness and equality for all. I promise that there will be no rules but the best rules. I promise to fight for your rights with the enemy . . . the school administration. I promise—"

"Promise to shut up," Badger growled.

"Boo! Down with the king!"

I looked at Carlos who chewed his lip and looked away.

No one seemed interested in fairness and equality for all. I opted for a different approach.

I grinned and shouted, "It's party time! With me as your king, life will be fun. Imagine an ice-cream machine in the cafeteria. Free ice cream. Or a pool table in the library? As future president of fifth grade, I'll listen to *your* ideas and make them come true."

Inside, I knew I wasn't telling the complete

truth, but I wanted to get their votes for student council president and win the election.

My classmates looked at one another. I knew they were thinking about all the things I had been famous for already that year—leading the fire-drill water balloon toss, and the bagpipe music that mysteriously played over the speakers during Principal Winthrop's morning announcements the first day of school. I was a natural leader.

Mr. Bailey's fifth-grade history class grinned and raised their sodas and milk cartons. "Long live King Justin."

"Huzzahs to King Justin," Willie added.

"*And* Queen Andrea," Priscilla said. "I'm not just here to look pretty, you know."

I sneered at her, then waved to the peasants in a royal manner, trying to ignore the fact that Carlos, Lester, and Badger were all glaring at me—the only ones who hadn't raised their drinks in salute.

Chapter 4

♛

Dreams to Follow

Future Politician's Rule #4—
Always have a plan.

I rolled my bike into the garage and leaned it against the dryer. It was the first time I'd gone home from school by myself in a long time. After my last class, I had waited for Carlos and Lester by my locker until the halls were quiet. I was surprised when I walked to the bicycle racks and saw that Carlos's black Schwinn and Lester's red fixer-upper were already gone.

I grabbed my bicycle and looked up to see Badger with this little kid who looked like he was in second grade. Badger had ahold of the kid's shirtsleeve and was leading him to the bus. I swallowed. What had this kid done to be Badger food? The kid wasn't crying or trying to get away, but why was a second grader hanging around Payton and getting on one of our buses with Badger? Before I could get the courage to confront them, they were on the bus and gone.

I hopped on my bike and rode home. Carlos and Lester and I always rode home together, honking matching air horns on our bikes. First we'd stop by Lester's house and feed his boa and listen to his newest jokes. Then, Carlos and I would ride to my house. Carlos would come inside for a grape jelly and cheese sandwich and tell me all about his last basketball game before going home.

They just didn't understand. A good politician couldn't play favorites. And to them, this was just a game, a cool project to do. But to me, it was my first real chance at being a leader.

"Dad? I'm home!"

I threw my books onto the sofa beside a pile of dirty clothes and went into the kitchen. I ignored the dishes piled in the sink. Dad had been ignoring them, too. So far, neither of us had been jumping to put them in the dishwasher since Mom had been away on her chef's training trip.

After grabbing a couple of granola bars and bottles of apple juice, I went out back to the shed behind the vegetable garden.

Dad had been working from home selling

insurance since Mom went to Houston for two months. She'd only been gone a week, but the house was beginning to look like a minor earthquake had hit. And I'd eaten nothing but undercooked eggs, overcooked chicken, and mushy meat loaf. I missed Mom's gourmet dinners and three-layer carrot cakes.

"You in there, Dad?" I shouted, kicking the door with my foot.

"Come in," a voice answered.

"Can't. My hands are full."

After a moment, the door opened. Dad stood in the doorway, rubbing his eyes. "Great, I could use a snack."

Inside the shed, I plopped into the faded purple beanbag chair that faced a small worktable. The shed was barely bigger than a large bathroom, but it was Dad's favorite spot. A pile of different kinds and sizes of wood stuck out of a cardboard box. Craft glues and paint bottles were stacked on a shelf beside Dad's table. The only chair in the room was the beanbag. That was mine. Dad preferred to stand when he worked.

I held out the snacks to Dad, set my juice on the floor, and tore open the granola bar.

"This really hits the spot," Dad said, after taking a long drink. "I didn't realize how late it was getting. I guess I should start supper. Tuna sandwiches with cream cheese okay?"

I shuddered. Leaning over to peer at the model on the worktable, I said, "Is that the one you're making for the library auction?"

Dad nodded. "I'm almost finished. Just need to get these hinges on the door and then I can load the animals inside."

He set down his juice and picked up the miniature carved door. I held my breath as he used a tiny screwdriver to put in screws I could barely see. His forehead wrinkled in concentration, and I knew he'd probably forgotten I was still there. He had a one-track mind when it came to his woodwork. Like me and politics.

I let out a loud burp. Dad looked up and grinned. "So, anything exciting happen at school today?"

I swallowed the last of my drink. "Yeah, I was crowned king."

Dad laughed. "And while you were at school, a two-inch-tall man from Mars came down and asked me to carve tiny wooden spaceships for their invasion of Pluto."

"Aw, Dad, you're goofy," I said. "Really, I was crowned king today. For two weeks. And creepy Andrea Carey is my queen."

Dad raised his eyebrows up and down. "Oh, and you have a queen, too? My, my, school wasn't this much fun when I was your age."

I groaned. "Gross, Dad. I'd rather have

Lester's cocker spaniel be my queen. Carlos and Lester are mad at me," I added.

Dad studied two bottles of brown paint. "Is that so?" he muttered.

"But that's okay," I said, pretending it would be. "Before this project's over, the whole school will know Justin Davies. I probably won't even need a campaign manager when I run for student council president. Voting is the Tuesday after this project ends, and by then I'll be a shoo-in. They'll want me to be president of the whole school, not just fifth grade."

The only sound was a woodpecker somewhere outside.

I cleared my throat. "Cool, huh?" I asked.

"Hmm, sure thing," Dad mumbled.

I got up to leave but stopped when Dad sighed. "What do you really think of the ark?"

"It's great."

Dad picked up a giraffe as small as his pinkie finger. "Think so? I'm happy the library asked me to donate something for the auction. They want to expand their children's book section and include a few more computers."

I touched the ark. Dad was great with his hands. I bet he could sell the things he made.

"Wish your mom could see it," he said.

I nodded. Mom liked hearing me talk about politics, too. We both missed her, but she had this chance to train at a great restaurant. She was a good chef and wanted to open her own restaurant someday.

I picked up the empty juice bottles. "I'm going to my room."

Dad waved a paintbrush at me. "Thanks for the snacks. Hey, maybe we could have those chicken legs in the refrigerator for dinner. I could try something new to marinate them in this time. Tomato soup? Or how about smothered in mushrooms and crunched-up potato chips?"

I winced and slipped out the door and hurried to my room. The king was in danger of being poisoned by his own father.

There were more important things to worry about. I only had two weeks to be king of fifth grade. There was a lot to get done. I stopped at the rack beside my door and straightened the hats I'd won from Mr. Bailey's class. I grabbed the General George Washington hat and put it on, then snatched a spiral notebook from my desk and lay across the bed.

At the top of the paper I wrote: *Kingly Goals*.

My number one goal was to show everyone what a great leader I could become. The first time I saw a PBS special about Abraham Lincoln when I was just eight, I wanted to be president. I started reading about other presidents, then other great leaders. Dad took me to a school board meeting once when they were trying to ban *Tom Sawyer* from the school library. It was fun watching the parents argue. And then I went to my first city council meeting and was hooked on politics.

The best way to show everyone my leadership strengths was to fulfill my promises. I guess I'd made a lot of them in my essay, but I'd find people who could help me make them happen. And there were lots of other things I could do that would show them I'd be the best choice for student council president. Our school's team is called the Payton Penguins. I wondered if the aquarium would loan us one for the football games. And the boys' gym equipment was a great angle. Everyone wanted it. Then, I'd have to find something the girls wanted. I needed their votes. If the teachers could vote, I'd bring doughnuts to the teachers' lounge every morning. But they couldn't, it was all up to the fifth graders.

I wrote:

1. Show the rest of the fifth graders real leadership and follow up on promises. (Call ice-cream machine companies. Call the zoo. Order pizzas for Pizza Party Fridays.)
2. Talk to every fifth grader and find out what he or she wants.

3. Be the best king ever so the voters will know I'll be the best fifth-grade president ever.
4. Agree humbly when everyone begs me to be student council president.

I tore out the sheet of paper and tacked it to my bulletin board, alongside the speech I wrote for the day I would be elected president of the United States.

"This is going to be a piece of cake with ice cream on top," I told my mirrored reflection. "Justin Davies, the next student council president. And there's no one to stand in my way."

Chapter 5

W

Leotards and Leadership

Future Politician's Rule #5—Never turn your back on your friends.

I called Carlos and Lester all weekend and twice before school Monday morning. They were always "too busy to talk." They wouldn't even answer the door when I went to their houses. I could see Carlos peeking out of his bedroom window when his little sister answered the door. She told me that Carlos had gone to Sweden for basketball practice.

But it wasn't until first-period PE that I realized just how upset my friends really were.

"Oh, great, I'm late." I clicked the lock on my bicycle chain. I'd spent half an hour trying to call my two *best* friends to apologize, and they hadn't even waited for me at our usual meeting spot. I ran into the locker room and saw that everyone else had already changed clothes and was in the gym. It took me three tries to get my combination right. The door swung open, bouncing off the next locker with a clang.

"Aargh!"

I stared into the locker. My gym clothes were gone. Instead, purple tights hung in one corner, like two wrinkled snakeskins. Baggy purple-and-black striped shorts had been placed where I usually kept my gray gym shorts. I pulled out the striped shorts and held them at arm's length. Silver sequins shone as the light hit them. Then I saw the red silk cape.

And the green, pointed-toed slippers.

I shoved the shorts back into the locker, slammed the door shut, and leaned against it.

I was already late—why not just skip first period? Or wear my jeans, shirt, and sneakers and get a zero for the day?

Then, the truth did a tap dance in my head. A painful tap dance. Only two people other than Coach Friedman knew the combination to my gym locker.

Carlos Mendoza and Lester Langford.

"I'll show them," I said. I would not be humiliated by jealous subjects.

Quickly, I undressed and put on the tights, shorts, cape, and shoes. I stomped my foot and stared at the curled toes shaking and bouncing on my feet. I had morphed into some kind of elf creature.

Turning, I swirled the cape around my shoulders and marched to the gymnasium.

Everyone stood around while the coach called roll. For a moment, I just watched from the doorway and stared at the group of fifth graders. I'd known most of them since first grade. Some of them weren't even in Mr. Bailey's history class, but everyone had heard about the project.

No. I just couldn't do it. I'd be laughed at.

But I'd never be forgotten.

Sometimes, a politician had to work a little harder to stand out in a crowd. All these guys were potential voters.

I moved out of the shadows.

"Hey, look!" someone shouted.

Like a slow-motion part of a movie, kids turned toward the door. I folded my arms, held my head high, and strolled toward them, twice tripping over the cape.

Eyes widened. Mouths dropped open. Then, the laughter started.

The small gym echoed with the sound of it. Nineteen fifth-grade boys went wild. A few doubled over and held their stomachs. Only one kid wasn't laughing.

Willie Fisher just stared, a frown scrunching

his face into a wrinkly prune. He rushed to my side.

"Justin . . . I mean, Your Majesty, do you think that this . . . um . . . costume is in good taste? I mean, consider how it looks to your people. Will they respect you in such attire?"

I kept walking.

"Willie, I'm king. I can dress any way I want."

"Hail, O Mighty King," Carlos said, bowing as I walked past.

Lester opened his mouth, then dropped to his knees, his face turning red as he sputtered and snorted. "Did you hear the one about the king who wore tights to gym class? He split his tights on his horse!"

"Funny, guys, real funny," I growled.

Coach Friedman glowered. He rubbed his bald spot and smirked. "I've heard about Mr. Bailey's little experiment. Well, this isn't history. It's physical education class and I'm ruler of all that you see in this gym. You're disrupting the class, Mr. Davies. Change into what the rest of the class is wearing."

I glanced at Carlos and Lester. I waited for them to tell me where they'd hidden my gym clothes.

They rolled their eyes toward the ceiling and began to whistle.

Badger gave me the biggest smile I'd ever

seen on his face. It was creepy. At least Andrea wasn't around to see me dressed like this.

Coach Friedman sighed. "Just lose the cape and the shoes. Let's get on with the class."

I unsnapped the cape, slipped off the green shoes, and shoved them into Willie's hands.

"Find someplace to put these," I ordered my knight.

We broke into teams for a game of basketball. Surprisingly, no one was dying to have a leotard-wearing king on his team, so I was last choice. Byron Hames frowned when he had last pick. I wasn't exactly known as the greatest basketball player in the fifth grade, but who could do well with equipment like ours? It wasn't easy to shoot at a tilted hoop.

"Come on, Your Majesty, pass me the ball," Byron yelled when I dribbled toward him. "Or do I need to curtsy?"

Carlos snickered. Lester grinned. I stared at my friends. My ex-friends.

After gym, I changed out of my costume and ran all the way to history class. I wanted to be the first in the room.

Quickly I explained to Mr. Bailey that Andrea's and my desks should be moved to the head of the room, facing the class, so that we could keep watch over the peasants. "It's a king's obligation to place his throne in the most strategic area of the castle, always at the head of the Great Hall."

41

Mr. Bailey tapped a pencil against his nose. "I suppose you're right. *Some* kings and queens shouldn't turn their back on their people. Go ahead, move the desks . . . just until the project is over."

I gave him a thumbs-up, then grabbed my desk and pulled it beside Mr. Bailey's. I shoved Andrea's on the other side of the teacher's desk. At least I wouldn't have to sit next to her.

The PTA was holding a special meeting that evening, and I intended to present myself as the "voice of my subjects." I had plans about how to make the school better, fairer, and definitely more democratic.

The gym equipment was the first thing on a long list of ideas for a better Payton. If I talked long and fast enough, the parents and teachers might be hypnotized by my political knowledge and my strong leadership. They might cheer. They might proclaim me class president without a vote. I could imagine how grateful they would be at finally finding a student worthy of such honor.

But first, I had to get even with Carlos and Lester.

When Andrea and Priscilla came into the room, I did a double take. Andrea glided into the room in a long gown.

White fur trimmed the red velvet gown and her braided hair was pinned up on the top of her head.

She looked cool. She looked regal. She looked at me.

"Why was my desk moved?" she asked, scowling at me.

Mr. Bailey explained my idea. Andrea nodded, then turned and smiled at me. "Perfect. We shouldn't have to sit with the peasants."

"Hey, what's going on?" Bobby Bryer shouted.

Everyone was standing around, staring at us as they walked into class. I had their attention. Time for a little lesson.

"Before class starts, I'd like to announce that Carlos Mendoza and Lester Langford have committed treason against my royalness and are to be thrown into the dungeon."

Lester gasped. Carlos yelled, "What?"

Mr. Bailey leaned back in his chair. "Sorry, boys. You heard the rules. Move your desks into the dungeon."

I watched my friends drag their desks and chairs across the room. We were even now.

With one last look at the dungeon's first guests, I began to make a mental list of what I would discuss at the PTA meeting. This was going to be a piece of cake.

Hadn't someone said, "Let them eat cake" during the French Revolution? I thought back on the studies that had led to this project, and I suddenly remembered that the person who said those words got her head chopped off in the end.

Chapter 6

♛

Assembling the King's Court

Future Politician's Rule #6—
A little bribery never hurts.

"**H**ey, Justin, I mean, Your Highness, how about sitting with us?"

I looked across the cafeteria and clutched my lunch tray. Was that really Danny Higgins asking me to sit with the Triangles? They were the most popular kids in school. Sixth graders.

"Sure," I mumbled, practically dropping my tray as I squeezed between the rows of tables.

The kids from my class looked at me with wide eyes. No one had been invited to sit with the Triangles since the group had formed back at Donna Park Elementary. If they let in a fourth, they'd be the Squares.

I moved past the empty seat between Willie and Andrea.

I didn't even look at Carlos and Lester as I walked by them. And I made a wide circle around Badger, who was busy writing in the red spiral notebook he always carried with him. Probably his hit list, I thought, wondering how many spots I had on that list.

"But . . . but . . . what about me?" Willie asked, half rising from his chair. "I'm your knight. We should sit together."

I rolled my eyes at him and walked on. Kevin Phillips bumped into me as we passed.

I turned when he kept walking. "Excuse me, but you just bumped your king without an apology. To the dungeon tomorrow."

Kevin's mouth dropped open. "Yes, Your Majesty," he mumbled.

I grinned. Kevin didn't grin back. But it was my right as king to expect respect from the peasants.

I plopped my tray beside Danny at the Triangles' table.

"Hi," I said, as if this wasn't the greatest honor I'd ever had but just another typical lunch.

Brandon Kelley snickered. "Howdy, King, slain any dragons lately?"

I snickered back. "Not yet. But I plan to."

I took a bite of my taco surprise, sure that everyone in the cafeteria was aware of my new fame.

Danny Higgins had lived all around the world. His father was a colonel in the air force. The last three years, they had lived in Texas. But Danny had pen pals from all the exciting places he'd lived—Japan, Germany, Hawaii, and more. Most of his pen pals were girls. Sometimes, he'd leave copies of the letters in the boys' bathrooms for guys to read. They were as mushy as the cafeteria meatballs. It made a guy want to throw up, but it was still cool.

Brandon Kelley's mother owned the Vid-O-Rama, the biggest video arcade in town. Brandon had the best birthday parties ever. They were always held in the arcade, with more food than anyone could eat and hours of free games. Of course, I had only heard the stories.

The third member of the Triangles was Marilee Cash. She wanted to be an actress someday. She was good, too. She had already been in three plays at the local theater and made a television commercial.

Danny and Brandon were both crazy about Marilee, but she could never decide who she liked best, so she hung around them both.

"I think this king thing is *so* amazing," Marilee said, giving me a sideways glance. She sighed. "I'm *sure* I could have played the part of *queen* if I were in Mr. Bailey's class."

I nodded. "You would have been great. Much better than Andrea."

Marilee leaned forward. "Of course, because I would *throw* myself into the part. I'd *live* it. I mean, you'd never know I hadn't been *born* in a castle."

Brandon and Danny nodded.

"That's why we asked you over," Danny explained, unzipping his leather flight jacket. "Marilee wants to be part of this thing, just for the acting practice. Could we, like, hang around until this class project is over?"

My jaw dropped.

"Everyone thinks this is just a project for Mr. Bailey's fifth-grade, second-period history class," I explained. "But it's really a chance for me . . . I mean, us kids, to be heard. As you probably know, I'm campaigning for student council president this year and any help I can get would . . ."

Brandon stuffed a handful of french fries in his mouth and mumbled, "Is there any rule against other kids being in your kingdom?"

I thought about it and decided there wasn't. "No, I guess not."

Marilee smiled. "Oh, *thank* you." She winked at me. "It wouldn't be *official*, of course, since we *aren't* in the same history class. Or grade. But,

I'd love, just *love,* to practice playing an older part. I could be your mother . . . still youthful and beautiful, yet *very* honored and respected."

"Yeah, sure, why not," I said. "What about you guys? What part will you play?"

Brandon patted Marilee's hand. Danny shot Brandon a warning look. "We'll be the queen mother's guards, of course."

I nodded. There was a way I could use the Triangles to help me. "Listen, when campaign week comes, I'd like to add to my posters, 'Justin Davies for President, endorsed by the Triangles.'"

Danny shrugged. "Sure, you help Marilee, and we'll let you use our name."

"Do you have any *exciting* plans?" Marilee asked me.

A tray dropped onto the table beside me. I looked up at Andrea, who looked down at me with a frown. "I'm sorry, but I must have missed my invitation to sit with you."

"You didn't miss it," I said.

Andrea sat down beside me anyway. She smiled at Marilee. "Sometimes, his majesty forgets about his better half."

I snorted.

Andrea leaned forward and gave Marilee a big smile. "Justin's leadership skills are more for leading a circus than the fifth grade. He's a boy, and they are uncouth and loud and wouldn't know good-smelling hand soap from a rotten egg. Imagine having lavender soap in the girl's rest rooms."

Marilee glanced at Andrea, then turned back to me. "You were about to tell us all about your *fabulous* plans for being noticed."

I glared at Andrea. She wasn't very couth herself, insulting me while I was sitting there. I swallowed the rest of my soda and grinned at Marilee. "There's a PTA meeting tonight at 7:00. I'm going to confront them about one of the issues on my presidential platform. It isn't right that Priscilla Ashworth-Cole's father buys all new PE equipment and builds a new gym for the girls and the boys get stuck with junk. It's favoritism, I tell you. I could go on and on . . ."

"Please don't," Danny said. "Save it for the parents and teachers. We'll meet you in front of the school at 6:45."

The three stood, picked up their trays, and walked away. I stared after them.

"The Triangles won't be the only ones at your little PTA party," Andrea said. She grabbed her tray and stomped back to Mr. Bailey's table.

The Triangles had given me a great idea. I'd planned to go to the PTA meeting alone. But what if I really made an entrance? A king with his entourage in tow.

After school, I waited at Carlos's locker.

"Well, if it isn't His-Royal-Pain-in-the-Asteroid himself," Lester said, banging his locker open.

Carlos leaned against the lockers and glared at me. "How about letting us out of the dungeon? Where's your team spirit?"

"Team spirit?" I said. "Who humiliated the king of fifth grade in gym class today? But that's okay, I forgive you. Look, you're still my best buddies, right? Mr. Bailey says that I can't let you out of the dungeon without Andrea agreeing. Andrea won't budge with you guys. But listen, I've got an idea how you can be part of all this."

"Yeah, what?" Carlos asked. He glanced at Lester and frowned.

"You can be my court jesters. You could clown around in Mr. Bailey's class and not get into trouble."

Lester grinned. "Hey, Jester Lester."

"What do you say?" I punched Carlos in the arm.

Carlos didn't look as honored as I'd hoped. He glared at me a moment, then shrugged. "Okay, we'll do it. And we'll get even with that Willie, too." He whispered something in Lester's ear and they both grinned at me. Before I could ask what they were whispering about, a shout caught my attention.

Down the hall, voices rose and fell in argument. I could hear one voice rising above the others. Andrea.

I weaved through the crowd of students.

Andrea stood in the center, hands on hips, frowning at Alison Foster and Christopher Poole. The two had been best friends since the first day of fourth grade.

Alison and Chris stared at Andrea with wide eyes. She walked around them, sweeping her long dress behind her.

"Aw, come on, Andrea," Chris said. "You've gone overboard with this queen thing."

Andrea waved her arms. "Listen, Mr. Bailey said that for the next two weeks, in class and out, as long as we're on the school grounds, you have to treat me like your queen."

Alison's face paled. "Please, Andrea. Chris and I *always* sit together."

I moved closer. Someone shouted, "Hey, make way. It's Old King Cole himself."

"What's the problem?" I asked.

Andrea sighed and explained, "I dropped my books. When I ordered this peasant to pick them up and carry them to the bus for me, he refused," she said, pointing at Chris. "I've sent him to the dungeon."

Chris shook his head. "But my bus goes the other way and it leaves before hers. That's dumb and I won't do it."

"It's not dumb if your queen asks you to do it," Andrea continued. "I told him that he'd be sitting in the dungeon until the project was over."

Alison said, "You promised to be a fair queen in your essay, Andrea Carey. Justin, don't you think she's being unfair?"

Everyone turned to stare at me.

Andrea moved closer to me and muttered, "Listen, you'd better stick up for me or I'll tell everyone you cheat on all your tests and will cheat to win student council president."

I sputtered, "Cheat? I'm an honest politician and will run my campaign and my presidency with honesty and fairness for all."

I turned to my friends for help. They weren't even paying attention to me. I jabbed Lester with my elbow.

Lester looked at the crowd. "Hey, I'm the court jester, everyone. Watch this!" He stood on his hands and walked toward me. "Oops," he yelped as his legs swayed. He toppled over, knocking Andrea into me. We landed in a pile onto the floor.

"Eek," she screamed, pushing Lester and me away as she scrambled up.

The crowd dissolved into applause and laughter. Andrea swatted at Lester with her purse. Carlos juggled pens and pencils. They weren't helping at all.

"What's the trouble here!" a voice boomed.

"Uh-oh," Carlos said. "It's Dragon Lady Winthrop."

The crowd scattered as the principal, her eyes wide and frizzed hair standing on end, descended on us. "Justin Davies! I should have known. To my office, now! And Miss Garey, I have come to expect this kind of chaos from Justin, but I'm surprised at you. Both of you follow me."

I looked around for support. Andrea and I were suddenly the only kids in the hall. My people had left me to face the dragon alone, with nothing but a traitorous queen at my side.

Chapter 7

♛

A Two-Headed Ogre and a Plan

Future Politician's Rule #7—Never let the enemy see you sweat.

Andrea and I sat in chairs across from Mrs. Winthrop's desk. I'd been in her office already this year more than I wanted to count, for getting on the loudspeaker to share my political views, speeches to the cafeteria ladies about the right for school prisoners to have food that tasted like food, and more. But this time, it wasn't my fault.

"Mrs. Winthrop, this isn't fair. I was trying to break up an argument. It's Andrea's fault. She started it," I said, pointing at her.

Andrea slapped my hand away. "I was handling things just fine until King Davies interrupted with his clown act." She folded her arms and sat straight in her chair. "I was only doing what Mr. Bailey said we could do for our class project."

Mrs. Winthrop mumbled, "Mr. Bailey." I didn't think he was her favorite teacher.

I raised my hand. Mrs. Winthrop turned cold dragon eyes on me. "Yes?"

"I never like to admit when a girl is right, especially Andrea, but Mr. Bailey did say we could put people in the dungeon."

Mrs. Winthrop picked up a purple ball and began squeezing it. "Yes, I did agree to allow this project to happen, but I will not tolerate screaming and wrestling in the hallways."

We both nodded and stood to go.

Mrs. Winthrop waved us back to our seats. "One more thing. I've been getting some strange messages. Tell me, Mr. Davies, why are Grady's Gym Equipment and The Discount Gym-mania faxing me price lists? And Miss Garey, why does the Spiritual Spa think the school would like a demonstration of their junior yoga class?"

I put my hands on her desk and leaned forward. "Mrs. Winthrop, as future fifth-grade class president, I have certain promises to keep for my constituents. Grady's and Gym-mania have the best prices around on gym equipment. But you don't have to decide right away, by the end of the day tomorrow would be fine."

Andrea shook her head. "We don't need more gym equipment. What we need is relaxation. Studies show that kids who are calm and relaxed do better on tests." She beamed at the principal and winked. "We girls need to stick together."

Mrs. Winthrop squeezed the tension ball a little harder. "There are procedures for change in this school. I won't be bullied or pushed around by students. If and when one of you becomes class president, I'll discuss ideas and we will go through proper forms and channels."

I gave her my best presidential smile. "I'm the next president of fifth grade," I explained. "After I'm through being king, that is."

"We'll see about that," Andrea said.

I glared at her. "What does that mean?"

"Out," Mrs. Winthrop said. She put her head on her desk and sighed.

Andrea jumped up and stomped out of the office. I walked to the door and looked back at Mrs. Winthrop. "Ma'am, when the man from the zoo comes, just tell him we need their biggest penguin for our mascot. He can stay in the pool and we'll feed him Fridays' fish sticks." I snapped my fingers. "Oh, and the pool contractor said he could start right away if you'll sign the papers."

Mrs. Winthrop groaned. I closed the door behind me.

I marched across the school grounds to where Carlos and Lester stood. "I ought to punch you guys for running off and leaving me. I've spent the last half hour in Winthrop's office."

Carlos dribbled a basketball behind his back. "So? We knew you could take care of yourself with the dragon lady."

He was right. I decided not to tell him about Andrea's part. "Listen, guys, tonight is your first assignment as my personal jesters."

Lester rubbed his hands together. "All right. What do we do? Can we dress in costume like Andrea did? Can I juggle? Walk on my hands?"

"Sure," I said. "Do whatever it takes to get us noticed. You guys can come in costume . . . but not me. I want them to take *me* seriously."

"Them, who?" Lester asked.

"The parents and teachers," I explained. "We're going to crash the PTA meeting with style. I've got my speech all ready."

"So, what will your court jesters do to liven things up?" Carlos asked. "I could show off my rim shot."

I waved my arms. "Whatever you want, except basketball. That's not what you call medieval. Just fade into the background when I'm ready to talk." I snapped my fingers. "Oh yeah, and there will be other people with us, too."

Carlos frowned. "Others? You mean Whiny Willie?"

"Of course, he's my knight. But even better, Danny Higgins and Brandon Kelley and Marilee will be a part of our group,"

"Wow," Lester said. "The Triangles? Hey, what do you get when you add together a triangle and a king? Give up? A square with a big mouth."

Carlos and I groaned.

"Yeah, the Triangles are a great addition to my court." Then I remembered Andrea's promise. Or was it a threat? "Andrea said she's coming, too."

"Yuck," Carlos said.

"Hey, guys, wait for me!"

We looked across the school yard to see Willie running toward us. "That guy's been following me around like a dog chasing a bone. He's full of ideas. They aren't so bad, but they aren't my ideas. Remember, we meet tonight at 6:30. In front of the school."

I turned to escape my knight when . . .

Wham!

I crashed into a wall.

The wall yelled at me.

"I'll flatten you, Davies!"

I looked up. And up. Badger Crabtree scowled down at me as if he were watching a bug he was thinking about squashing. "Uh, sorry, Badger. I didn't see you standing there," I said, backing away. Good grief, how could anyone miss Badger?

He was a walking mountain. A two-headed ogre with one brain.

Badger poked me in the chest. "Just watch it, Your Majesty, or we'll be singing 'The king is dead, long live the new king.' Me!"

Willie caught up with us, gasping for air. "You can't threaten him. Why . . . he'll throw you into the dungeon for treason."

I grabbed Willie's arm and whispered. "What are you doing!"

"I'm only protecting your honor like a good knight should," Willie said. He whispered out of the corner of his mouth, "The future president of the student council should stand up to bullies in front of his voters."

He motioned toward the other kids standing outside the school. They were watching me. I didn't want them to see me become King-Of-Bruises.

Carlos and Lester backed away. Why weren't they protecting their king?

Badger growled. "I'd just like to see you try and throw me into the dungeon." He clenched and unclenched his fists.

I tried to swallow, but my throat had gone dry.

Badger stuck his face next to Willie's. "Stay out of my way or I'll turn your days into one long knight-mare."

Badger bent over to pick up his notebook.

After shaking his fist at me once more, he walked across the street, growled at two kids on skates, then disappeared around the corner.

I let out my breath. "Are you nuts? That guy could ground us into medieval pulp. I saw him leading a poor second grader to his doom yesterday."

I quickly told Willie about the PTA meeting. Willie congratulated me on my interest in school affairs, then bowed and walked away.

"Come in costume!" I yelled to my departing knight.

I rode ahead of Carlos and Lester. They were too busy talking about their plans to entertain the parents at the PTA meeting to pay attention to me.

"Don't forget who's king," I reminded them as I sped away toward Willie.

Inside the front door, I tripped over the mail that had overflowed the hall table and onto the floor. Someone should pick it up. I glanced at Mom's ficus. Weren't we supposed to be watering it?

"Dad!" I yelled. "There's mail all over the floor. What's for dinner? I need to eat early tonight."

I heard him mumbling in the next room. Smoke drifted out from the kitchen. "Burned again," Dad's voice said between coughing spasms.

I decided I wasn't hungry.

I hurried to my room to work on my speech. It had to be perfect. In just two hours I was going to have the parents' and teachers' full attention. At least, that was the plan.

I pulled on my T-shirt with the American flag on the front. Below the flag in bold black letters were the words *Have You Hugged a Politician Today?*

Somewhere beneath the pile of towels and clothes on my floor were clean socks, but I didn't have time to look. I grabbed the least dirty ones and yanked them on. No one was going to smell my feet. They would be too busy being awed by my powerful words.

I reread my speech for the fifth time, then looked at my watch. "Uh-oh, I'm going to be late."

"Where are you going?" Dad asked as I hurtled down the stairs, three steps at a time.

I watched him carefully glue tiny cannons to a model ship. Dad did his woodwork in the shed, but he loved sitting on the living room floor and building ships from kits. The mantel over the fireplace was a sea of ships.

"I've got a meeting at school," I explained. "Carlos and Lester will be there, too. It's a political deal, Dad."

"Oh, some type of government club? Well,

61

I'm glad to see you getting involved. But try to let some of the other kids talk, too." He picked up a tiny pirate flag and gently glued it above the crow's nest on the model. "Get a ride home with Carlos's or Lester's parents, okay? It'll be dark when you're done. I'd better try to clean the kitchen a little if we want any more meals while your mom is gone."

I nodded. "Okay. Everyone might stop and get ice cream after the meeting."

"Fine. But be home by 8:30. It's a school night." Dad seemed to hesitate. "Maybe I should just go with you."

"No! I mean, you'll just be bored." I held my breath until Dad went back to work.

I pointed to Mom's ficus tree in the corner. It looked a little droopy and the leaves didn't seem as green as before.

"Uh, Dad, didn't you promise to water all Mom's plants?"

"Hmmm?" He mumbled.

I shrugged. Dad was the one who promised Mom, not me. I had a campaign to run.

I ran out the door and hopped on my bike. All the way to the school grounds I rehearsed my speech. This time, Dragon Lady Winthrop would take me seriously. This time she would understand that my intentions were. . . .

I skidded my bike to a stop. "Wow!"

It looked as if someone was making a movie about King Arthur on the front lawn. A crowd of costumed kids stood there laughing and talking. The only thing missing was a dragon. And if Mrs. Winthrop showed up before I was ready for her, the cast would be complete.

Chapter 8

♛

Royal Chaos

Future Politician's Rule #8—Never lose control of your staff.

I let my bike fall to the ground as I climbed off. Everyone turned toward me.

"It's about time!" Andrea shouted. She wore the same long gown as before, but this time, she had a crown on her head. She walked toward me, lifting her skirt to reveal pink high-top tennis shoes. "So, what's the big plan? I'm going to ask Mr. Bailey for extra credit for this."

Extra credit? We'd be lucky if we didn't get detention.

Andrea studied me a moment and wrinkled her nose. "Why aren't you in costume? And what's the big idea of making Carlos and Lester your court jesters? Mr. Bailey didn't say anything about having jesters," she said, glaring into my face.

"Listen, I don't have to ask Mr. Bailey about everything. I am the king," I said.

Andrea adjusted her crown. "Yeah? And I'm the queen. Don't forget it."

Priscilla fussed over Andrea's hair while a crowd of other girls swirled around them, showing off their own costumes.

"Who told you that you could bring your own groupies?" I asked.

"They're my court," Andrea said. "I'm here to ensure that my ideas get heard."

Carlos juggled a dog's squeaky basketball against my head.

"Getting into the PTA meeting was my plan," I reminded her. What kind of ideas was she talking about?

"Hey, Mighty King, let's get this show on the road," Lester said. He did a cartwheel and landed on Andrea's foot.

"Ow, watch it!"

I laughed at his costume. Lester pranced around, modeling his jester outfit. "Don't you like it? I made it myself."

He wore an old clown costume that was too small. I could see the red patches where Lester's mother must have let out the seams. The elastic legs came only to his knees. Below, he wore red, white, and blue striped kneesocks.

"Oh, man," I said. "Where's that ringing coming from?"

Lester pointed to his feet. His black tennis shoes had little bells tied along the shoelaces that jangled whenever he walked.

I slapped him on the back. "You're sure to make people laugh."

He just turned away and walked over to Carlos.

Marilee Cash floated through the crowd. Her costume looked as authentic as Andrea's. She even wore a white wig and a small gold crown with red stones. "My son, how *wonderful* to see you. I have been abroad this past year and have missed the *radiance* of your smile. Come, give your *mother* a kiss."

I moved toward her. Danny and Brandon stepped between us. They wore black jeans and black shirts. "Pardon us, O King, but if you toucheth her lips, we'll breaketh your nose," Brandon said with a broad smile.

I opened my mouth to remind them that it was all a part of the class project when I heard a loud *Clank! Clank! Clank!*

"What's that?" I whirled around. Across the school grounds, a large silver object moved toward us. My mouth dropped open at the sight of my knight inside a metal trash can. The bottom had been removed for Willie's legs. Thick rope was looped over his arms to hold it up, and foil was wrapped around his legs and arms. Willie held the can's metal lid like a shield. He'd even painted a badly drawn picture of my face on the lid.

"Your Majesty," he said. "I think it's time we went into the PTA meeting. They are about to begin."

Lester shouted, "It's Sir Trash-A-Lot!"

I groaned. And Willie talked to *me* about looking silly in front of the voters?

Carlos, whose costume consisted of tie-dyed scarves wrapped around the legs of his jeans and a felt jester hat I'd brought him from my trip to Six Flags Amusement Park last year, burst into laughter. "Hey, Willie, put a lid on it, will you?"

"Yeah," Lester added. "Maybe we should recycle him. How many whiny Willies does it take to make a trash can into a corny costume? One."

Willie scowled.

I grabbed him and pointed to the noisy group in the school yard. "Who *are* all these kids?"

He waved his arms, looking more like a robot than a knight. "You wanted an unforget-table entrance into the PTA meeting. I invited a few people to help. Konrad over there is your food taster. Then there are the Stuard twins. They are your official door openers. And all those

67

giggly girls—Michelle, Ashley, Brittany, Michala, and Kaitlyn are Andrea's ladies-in-waiting."

Willie pulled a large red bathrobe and a wooden sword from inside his can. "Um, Justin . . . I mean, Your Majesty? You really *must* wear some sort of costume."

"No way," I said. Then, it hit me. Every king needed royal robes. And a king going into battle needed his sword. I took the bathrobe and wrapped the arms around my shoulders while Willie safety pinned them to my shirt. Someone from the crowd ran forward holding a torn couch cushion. A cardboard crown from a kid's pizza restaurant sat on top. I snatched it up, waved the kid away, and dropped the crown on my head.

With a swirl of my robe, I held my sword high and shouted, "Onward!"

Andrea stepped in front of me. "This isn't a one-ruler kingdom, you know. I have some demands, too."

I had a bad feeling about Andrea's sudden interest in school issues. There wasn't anyone who could outtalk Justin Davies, though. I was in complete control of this crowd.

I gave Andrea a bow and moved to the front of the crowd. Andrea marched to my side, and we led the procession up the steps and through the front door. Down the hall I could hear Mrs. Winthrop calling the PTA meeting to order.

Chapter 9

♕

My Kingdom for a Better Horse

Future Politician's Rule #9—Leave
your staff at home.

I adjusted my crown and led the way to the
music room where the PTA meetings were
held. The crowd filled the hallway with a
sea of color.

I smiled at my queen, her knight, my knight,
the two jesters with their homemade costumes,
my white-haired queen mother and her guards,
the food taster (I still wasn't too sure I liked the
idea of someone sampling my food before I
did), the Stuard twins (who opened every door I
walked past), and the assorted ladies-in-waiting
and guys wearing wooden swords who pushed

their way down the hall. Were there really this many kids in fifth grade? Voters. Lots of voters.

I peeked through the small window in the music room door. Mrs. Dollahan, the PTA president, stood beside the piano, waving her hands and talking quickly. Her hair hung in braids that touched her shoulders. She wore a jean skirt, denim blouse, and dangly earrings that bounced when she moved her head. Even the earrings were shaped like a pair of jeans. Sondra Dollahan said her mom was a hippie from way back.

". . . And although the police hope to eventually find the vandals who destroyed our lovely trees, bushes, and flowers, we must find a way to replace them. It's our duty to the school to beautify it, to leave a legacy to our grandchildren of oxygen-giving plants. Tonight, we are asking for your suggestions on ways to raise money for this worthy project. *And* volunteers. Any ideas?"

I slapped my hands over my ears as a screech echoed around the room. One of my followers had snuck into the room and grabbed a trumpet from a nearby shelf.

"Hear ye, hear ye!" he shouted, saluting the crowd with the trumpet. "The king has arrived." He put the trumpet to his mouth and blew again, squawking like a strangled goose.

The Stuard twins opened the door. Parents

and teachers turned in their seats to gawk at the costumed crowd filling the room.

When I passed by Mr. Bailey, he covered his face with his hands and leaned forward in his chair.

"Excuse me, young man . . . *children,*" Mrs. Winthrop said, jumping from behind the podium. "We're in the middle of a PTA meeting. You'll have to do your play rehearsal somewhere else."

I took a deep breath and marched to the front of the room. The rest of my troupe stood in the aisles and in the back of the room.

"This isn't a rehearsal for a play," I explained. "It's Mr. Bailey's class project. I'm king, and Andrea is queen."

Andrea swept up the center aisle, curtsied to the crowd, and sat in a chair near where I was standing. Priscilla hurried to her side, followed by the ladies-in-waiting, who brought Andrea a cushion for her back.

Mr. Bailey slid further down into his seat.

"I have been chosen to speak for my people," I said.

"Yeah!" several kids shouted.

"I have many things of great importance I must discuss with the leaders of this school," I said. "And you are our leaders, here to serve our young minds."

Mrs. Winthrop's face turned splotchy shades

of red and purple—unusual colors for a dragon, I thought.

Mrs. Dollahan wrung her hands. "We really must stick to the schedule."

"Let the boy talk," Lester's father said. Other parents nodded, seeming to enjoy the show.

Andrea jumped from her seat, nearly knocking her ladies-in-waiting over like bowling pins.

"The queen has something to say, too. I want equal time to make my own demands."

I stepped in front of her.

"Me first, this was my idea," I said, bowing to the room full of parents and teachers. "I'd like to talk about the horrible condition of the boys' gym equipment, the inclusion of an ice-cream machine in the cafeteria, a party in the class-rooms on our birthdays, a video game center, and . . . oh yes, a foosball table in the back of the library."

Mrs. Winthrop groaned.

Marilee Cash walked grandly around the room, followed by her two guards. She put her hands over her heart and shouted, "How *proud* I am this night of my son, my one and only son, the king. His words *fall* like the rain, like *showers* of wisdom, like—"

"Like I haven't started yet," I said.

Pulling a stack of note cards from my pants pocket, I began my speech when a *clang* followed by a crash caused everyone to turn toward the back of the room.

Willie rolled around on the floor in his trash-can armor while two parents struggled to lift him to his feet.

I cleared my throat and began again. "Every girl and boy in this school should have equal rights. It's important to make sure that we are happy while we learn."

"Woohoo!" a voice shouted.

I waved in a kingly manner. "Therefore, herewith, and all that stuff, as king, I decree that these things must be considered immediately. Ice cream is a dairy product, right? It builds strong bones. So why isn't there a soft-serve machine in the cafeteria? I've seen teachers carry birthday cakes into the teachers' lounge. And video games stretch the imagination and help our coordination. Last of all, the boys have the right to gym equipment that is as good as the girls'."

Laughter came from the back of the room. Several of the parents were standing and watching something. I stood on my toes and saw Lester juggling cookies while Carlos reached out, grabbed one, and crammed it in his mouth. The kids at the back of the room, and some of the parents, were applauding them.

I glanced at Andrea and the girls fussing around her.

"Stop it," Andrea said, pushing them away.

She tugged at Mrs. Dollahan's arm. "Excuse me, but I'd like to make my speech now."

Mrs. Dollahan's eyes widened and she backed away.

I glared at the Stuard twins who were practicing opening and closing the door at the back of the room. I scowled at Marilee who was bowing and passing out autographed napkins.

I'd lost my audience.

Parents' heads turned from side to side, trying to keep up with the chaos. A few looked angry. Andrea's father fussed over his wife, who looked as if she might faint. But most of the parents laughed or applauded as if every PTA meeting should come with its own floor show.

I cleared my throat. I cleared it again, louder this time. I waved my arms.

"I want silence!"

Everyone in the room turned to look at me.

Andrea smiled at me. "Thank you, I'll take over now." She pulled a piece of paper from her dress sleeve and cleared her throat.

"I have a few ideas I'd like to discuss now, they shouldn't take more than an hour. First of all . . ."

I pounded on the podium. "I wasn't finished talking. It isn't polite to interrupt."

Mrs. Dollahan coughed and pointed at me. "Exactly, young man, as I was saying before you children burst in—"

"Look at the unfairness in the PE classes," I said quickly. I was going to finish my talk even if I had to stand on my head to get everyone's attention. "The girls' equipment is new and modern. The guys are stuck with old and tacky junk. We have a mini-tramp, they have a full-size trampoline. Our even bars are uneven. Our horse is a nag. Our balance beam is lopsided. Our wrestling mats are thinner than my mom's pancakes. Our medicine ball needs a doctor."

I paused for dramatic effect. "In two weeks, the fifth graders of Payton will be choosing their student council for the year. And who is the best candidate for president?" I pointed around the room, then quickly tapped my chest. "Me, that's who!"

Suddenly, my throat felt like a dry well, my mouth like cotton. I tried to continue, coughed, then had a choking fit.

A kid pushed his way through the crowd. "Let me by, please!" A canteen swung from around his neck. He grabbed a paper cup off a table of coffee and cookies. After pouring a brown liquid from the canteen, he shoved the cup into my hand. "Here, King Justin."

I had never even met this kid before. New followers were appearing everywhere I turned. "Who are you supposed to be?" I asked.

The kid grinned. "I'm your cupbearer."

Konrad Beasley leaped forward to grab the

cup. "Your kingliness, I have to taste this before you do."

I ignored Konrad and gulped down the liquid. Slimy water that tasted like blenderized fish sticks slid down my throat. I choked, spitting out half the drink on Mrs. Winthrop's shoes. I sniffed the cup and wrinkled my nose. "What *is* this stuff?"

"Water. I filled my canteen from the fishpond in front of the school."

"Fish water! Ugh!" I wiped my mouth on the bathrobe-cape.

Konrad backed away. "Yuck! I'm out of here."

Andrea jumped up and shoved me aside. "Well, how about the girls? I am Queen Andrea, and I represent the girls at Payton. We have demands, too. We want perfumed towels in the girls' showers, designer gym suits, waiters in the cafeteria, phones in our lockers, and—"

Mrs. Dollahan interrupted. "Fine speeches, but what we *really* need are new trees, shrubs, and flowers to replace those destroyed. If anyone has any ideas on how we can raise the money, please see me after the meeting to form a committee." She glanced around the room. After looking at her watch, she shrugged and said, "Considering the interruptions and the time, we'll just declare this meeting over."

"Hey," I said. "What about my great ideas?" I glanced around the room. "Don't forget, vote for me for your fifth-grade student council president!"

Mrs. Winthrop bent to wipe the fish water from her shoes, then stood to face me. "If you are voted president of student council . . ." She turned away and I could have sworn she whispered to Mrs. Dollahan, "I'll resign and become a forest ranger!" She looked at me with a forced smile. "If it happens, you can bring me a well-thought-out, reasonable list of suggestions."

She glanced at Andrea. "And Miss Carey, the school cannot afford lighted mirrors in the rest rooms, so please stop giving my phone number to contractors and bathroom remodelers."

Andrea shrugged. "I am only a voice for my people."

The principal waved us both away. "The show is over."

"You haven't heard the last of this," I warned. "I'll be hanging around like a bad report card." I turned to motion to my royal entourage. "C'mon, let's lead the invasion of Darryl's Ice Cream across the street."

As we spilled out into the hallway, we were met by Mr. Bailey. "Well, this little project has become quite a big event," he said. "I'm glad to see you kids getting involved with school problems, but this isn't the way. You were being disruptive, not helpful. If you do something like this again, we'll be talking after-school detention."

"Mr. Bailey," I asked. "How does a king or president or average kid get anyone to listen?"

Mr. Bailey shrugged. "If you're going to be a politician, you've got to learn how to be tactful. Timing is important, too." He turned and walked away.

At Darryl's Ice Cream, I sat by myself in a corner and dug my spoon into a hot-fudge banana split. Willie sat at the next table, watching me as if I might need protection from some crazed ice-cream server.

Everyone told me that the PTA meeting had been a blast and could they do it again, please? Everyone except Konrad Beasley.

"That fish water was gross. As my taster, you should have protected me," I said. "You're in the dungeon tomorrow."

He glared at me and grabbed my banana split.

"Let go," I ordered. I fought for control of my ice cream. Konrad took my spoon and ate a big bite of my ice cream, shoved the rest of the banana split onto the table, and left. Another angry peasant.

I chopped at the bananas on the table. What had I done wrong at the PTA meeting? It wasn't supposed to be fun. It was supposed to be productive.

I heard giggles from behind me and turned to see Andrea standing on a chair. Priscilla tapped a spoon against a soda glass. "Please, your queen is about to speak."

Everyone stopped talking, even the people dipping ice cream behind the counter.

"King Justin has given me a wonderful idea. I am announcing that I have decided . . ." Andrea looked at me and smiled.

I had a feeling I wasn't going to like what she had to say.

". . . to run for president of the fifth-grade student council."

Willie's mouth dropped open. Everyone stared at me.

Andrea gave me a smile. "What do you say about that, Your Majesty?"

What could I say? The king was speechless.

Chapter 10

♕

Life Isn't Fair . . . Love, Mom

Future Politician's Rule #10— Watch out for overzealous groupies.

Andrea's surprise announcement was the worst thing I could have heard. Being queen had gone to her head. If I didn't do something, I was going to lose votes. No one else had dared to run against me. Until now.

The day after the PTA meeting, the Stuard twins were late to their classes because they were waiting at each of my classes to open the door for me. My food taster stole my lunch. Twice. It got so bad that I even let Willie act as my bodyguard. He wasn't much of a bodyguard, but once he started dancing around me like a nerd force field, there were fewer people bugging me. Unfortunately, they started bugging everyone else.

When Aaron Petrey burst into the teachers' lounge and shouted, "My king demands all your desserts for taxes!" I got a lecture from Mr. Bailey, who had gotten a lecture from the dragon lady.

After lunch, Willie and I walked to English class.

"When you are student council president, your voice will be a voice of reason," Willie said. "But I'm afraid the people believe you are going to keep all your promises."

"I can try," I said. I glanced at the kids pushing past us to get to class. Some waved at me and bowed.

Willie shook his head. "But trying isn't doing. I've always felt that a good leader doesn't make a bunch of promises just to get votes or make people happy, he makes a plan. You should pick one of your promises and spend all your time making it happen. You should use this time as king to make friends, not enemies."

I stopped walking. "Willie, if I don't say I'll do things, Andrea will, and they'll vote for her."

Willie pointed down the hall. "Maybe. But look at all the enemies she's creating along the way."

Andrea stood with a group of her friends, Priscilla and her "court," who followed her everywhere.

Charles Peterson was backed up against a locker like a cornered rat.

"The dungeon for you," Andrea shouted, pointing in his face.

He clutched his books and slid along the lockers until he was past Andrea and her court.

"What did *he* do?" I asked.

Andrea waved me away. "He spilled macaroni and cheese on my royal sweater. And I'm going to find that Gina Ribell, too. She laughed at me when I did a crooked cartwheel in PE."

She hurried down the hall, shouting at Gina who was ducking behind the water fountain.

Willie nudged me. "I'm telling you, Justin, that girl is out of control. And, I'm sorry to say this, Your Majesty . . . you are losing votes as fast as Andrea."

Willie could be the most annoying and irritating guy around. But he was also right.

The dungeon was beginning to fill. I had to send Aaron; he'd spoken for the king without asking permission. And Tasha Benson wouldn't let me cut in the lunch line last week. I was king and shouldn't have to wait in lines like the peasants. I helped her move her desk into the dungeon, and she didn't even thank me.

Now the "dungeon kids" were glaring at me in the hallways and some of the other peasants were beginning to look unhappy.

After sixth-period science, I headed out of

the school when Mrs. Winthrop stopped me. "Come with me, please," she said.

I wondered which vendor I'd called was bothering her now. I'd called so many, I couldn't even remember which ones promised to come to the school.

Andrea stood outside the office.

"In my office, both of you," Mrs. Winthrop said.

We followed her inside. It was like a bad rerun.

A man in gray overalls and a hard hat stood in one corner of Mrs. Winthrop's office. Telephone cords were looped around his arm, and he was holding a clipboard.

Mrs. Winthrop sat in her chair and folded her arms. "So, which one of you ordered sixty-three phones for the fifth-grade lockers?"

I raised my eyebrows and looked at Andrea. Her face reddened.

"I did, Mrs. Winthrop," Andrea said. "But just think of the great communication we could have with one another? And teachers could call students and leave messages. Wouldn't that be helpful?"

Mrs. Winthrop waved to the man from the phone company. He held out the clipboard. Mrs. Winthrop grabbed it and shoved it in Andrea's face. "Here's a bill for $1,328.56, Miss Carey. Did you plan on paying for this?"

Andrea shook her head. "Oh no, I was thinking that maybe you and the teachers might donate some of your salaries to such a worthy cause."

Mrs. Winthrop gasped. She gave the clipboard back to the frowning man. "I'm sorry, there's been a mistake. This order was unauthorized."

"You'll be hearing from my boss, lady!" the man shouted as he stormed out of the office.

Mrs. Winthrop lectured us both for ten minutes. She rubbed her forehead, took two aspirin, and told us to leave.

All the way home from school, I imagined someone was following me. Lester had after-school detention for refusing to do his math test on the grounds that he didn't need math to do cartwheels for the king. Carlos said he had basketball practice, even though I knew he'd just finished practice for the day.

How could my friends, my best friends, just dump me like this? Being king of fifth grade was the best, but it would be more fun with my best friends in my corner.

When I got home, I unlocked the front door and slipped inside, peeking through the window once more to make sure no one was there.

Dad tapped me on the shoulder. I jumped a foot.

"There's a letter from your mother on the kitchen table," Dad said.

I watched him pile papers into a briefcase. "New client?"

Dad nodded. "The parents of a classmate of yours, in fact. The Ashworth-Coles. They're unhappy with their insurance and are switching to my company. It's quite an honor that my boss asked me to take them."

I wrinkled my nose. "Prissy Priscilla's parents? Ugh. Rich and snooty."

"If you're going to be a politician someday, it would be wise to make friends with a few people like the Ashworth-Coles. After all, you've got to raise campaign money," Dad said. "Besides, Priscilla is a very polite young lady."

"Of course she's polite to you. You're an adult."

Dad laughed. "I'll be home in an hour. Call Mrs. Russell next door if you need anything," Dad said. "There's a warm pizza on the table and a salad in the refrigerator. Please don't skip the salad. Oh, and would you water the ficus tree?"

I waited until I heard his car drive away before going into the kitchen. After searching the cabinets, I found a clean coffee mug and poured a glass of orange juice. Mom's letter was lying on top of a pile of catalogs and bills.

Dear Justin,
    I hope things are going well. I miss you. Thanks for your e-mail. I still prefer sending

a letter, though. It sounds like you've got an interesting teacher. I'm sure you're a wonderful and fair king. How are your grades? I hope this project isn't causing you to neglect your schoolwork.

Is Dad feeding you okay? Are you helping each other with the chores around the house? Don't forget to take care of my roses outside and the hall ficus tree.

I wish you could be here with me. It's very exciting in Houston, but you and your Dad will be spending Christmas here. My boss at Chantilly Lace Bistro called. He still wants me to finish my training here, but I may have to hold off awhile on running my own kitchen. I guess life isn't fair all the time. I'll say good-bye for now. Kisses and hugs.

Love, Mom

I stared at the letter. There are always obstacles in life, Dad liked to say. But I wasn't going to let my own obstacles stop me from winning student council president.

A great politician convinces people to believe in him and his ideas. What I needed was something that showed everyone what a strong and brave leader I would be on the student council. I needed a major political event.

Chapter 11

♔

Baa, Baa, Badger, Please Don't Break My Face

Future Politician's Rule #11— Bullies and plans don't mix.

"**O**ut of my way, Tin Man." Badger barged into the classroom, knocking Willie to the floor.

I had been talking to Edgar Starkey. His dad knew a guy who knew a guy who had a friend who owned a sporting goods store. It never hurt to make friends with people in high places.

I tried to ignore what was going on between Badger and Willie, but then I saw Badger give Willie another shove as soon as Willie stood.

"Hey," Willie said to Badger. "I'm the king's

87

knight and expect to be treated with respect. I would like an apology, or you're going to be sorry."

My mouth dropped open. Willie never, never, *ever* threatened anyone.

"Ooh, the little knight's going to knock my block off," Badger said. He shook all over, then collapsed into his chair, snorting with laughter.

Willie stood his ground. "I'm waiting for that apology."

I held my breath. Where was Mr. Bailey? What had happened to the old Willie? He seemed more confident since this project had started.

Badger jumped from his seat, causing several kids nearby to fall out of their chairs in their hurry to move away.

"Listen, if you're not out of my face by the time I count to ten, I'm going to punch you into next week. Got it?"

For a moment, Willie's eyes widened. I let out my breath and smiled. Willie had regained his senses and was going to back down. Then he puffed up like a bullfrog, looked Badger in the eye, and said, "I didn't know you could count that high."

Badger opened and closed his mouth like a fish gasping for air. He doubled up his fist and pulled it back.

"Stop!" I yelled, running across the room.

Badger lowered his hand. "And who's gonna make me? You? King-Of-Nothing?"

"Come on, Badger," I pleaded. "You're nothing more than a frightened kid searching for his place in the world. Political leaders have dealt with bullies before, and we understand that you're just crying out for help . . ."

Badger sputtered a laugh. "Your long-winded speeches don't impress me. I'd be just as happy to squash two wimps for the price of one." He raised both his hands and curled them into fists.

Andrea pounded on her desk. "I will not have fighting in my kingdom! When I am president of the student council, fighting will be outlawed. It's much too noisy."

I glared at her. "When who's president of the student council?"

She stuck her tongue out at me and looked away.

"Hey!" someone shouted. "Mr. Bailey's coming."

Everyone scrambled to their seats. I grabbed Willie by his jacket and dragged him to his chair, then ran to my seat beside Mr. Bailey's desk.

As Mr. Bailey walked in, Christopher Poole jumped to his feet. "Mr. Bailey, I have a complaint about our project." He stood beside his desk at the back of the dungeon.

Mr. Bailey glanced at Andrea and me and crossed his arms. "Well, it's your kingdom. It's the ruling power's duty to deal with the problems in the realm."

I nodded. "Of course, everyone is equal in *my* kingdom. Everyone has the right to complain, though I can't imagine why anyone would. After all, Andrea and I have strived to do as we said we'd do if we were king and queen."

Christopher shook his head. "Yeah, we may all be equal, but some are more equal than others! You promised to be fun. This is as much fun as long division. All you do is make campaign speeches and promises you can't keep." He pointed at Andrea. "And Andrea promised to be fair. I was thrown in the dungeon just because I wouldn't carry her books and miss my bus. But Badger threatens and insults our king and gets away with it. Is that fair?"

"No!" shouted several kids, mostly the ones in the overcrowded dungeon. It had already been enlarged twice, and there were more desks inside than out.

Mr. Bailey shook his head at me. "You have a revolt brewing. You'd better deal with it and make a decision." He looked at the other students. "Remember, class, this is only a project. I expect you to behave. But, Justin and Andrea, you have to listen to your subjects and settle disputes."

I looked at Badger. He smiled and punched a fist into the palm of his hand.

"Uh . . ." I said.

"Well?" Christopher shouted.

"Your Majesty," Willie whispered to me. "It's time to act."

I swallowed. My mouth opened. I knew what I had to do, even if I was signing my own pounding warrant. No long speech this time—just a short decree. "I hereby order that Badger Crabtree be thrown into the dungeon," I mumbled. I'd shown them authority and leadership.

I'd shown them a dead king.

Badger grabbed his desk and chair and noisily dragged it into the dungeon. The other inmates scooted their desks back, giving him as much space as they could. Badger's face turned as red as an apple and his eyes squinted at me until they were fiery slits.

I studied my fingernails closely.

Mr. Bailey pointed at Badger. "Everyone follows the rules of the project. And I'd better not hear of any fights. Okay, put your books away and take out a pencil. No talking until everyone completes today's quiz." He wrote three questions on the board:

1. When did the American Revolution begin and end?
2. When did the French Revolution begin and end?
3. Compare the American and French Revolutions and what made the people in both

situations rise up against their leaders/oppressors.

I huddled over my test paper. I was terrible at remembering dates, and I didn't want to think about leaders being overthrown. I glanced at Badger and saw his You're-a-Pile-of-Dog-Meat-in-a-Hamburger-Bun look.

When the lunch bell rang, Mr. Bailey collected the test papers. I hadn't even finished half the page.

"You'd better eat in the courtyard today," Lester suggested, nodding toward Badger. "Or maybe the basement."

I agreed. I was surprised when Carlos and Lester walked past me and out the door. I walked alone to my locker to get my lunch. Several kids bowed when I passed. I waved at them, trying to get back into the spirit of being king, but the fun had disappeared.

I pushed the doors open and strolled into the courtyard where kids sat on benches to eat their lunch. Because the courtyard was inside the school, the lone tree in a grassy corner was the only tree that hadn't been destroyed by the vandals.

Priscilla and Andrea giggled as they ran past me, handing out pieces of paper to everyone. Priscilla shoved one in my hand.

QUEEN ANDREA FOR STUDENT COUNCIL PRESIDENT!

VOTE FOR THE SWEETER, PRETTIER CANDIDATE. WHAT DO YOU WANT THE REST OF YOUR FIFTH-GRADE YEAR TO BE LIKE? COME TO LOCKER 132 AND WRITE DOWN YOUR NEEDS. I AM HERE FOR YOU!

I stared at the flyer. Andrea was going to be trouble. With friends like Priscilla Ashworth-Cole, she had people in high places whose rich father could make Andrea's promises come true.

Why was Andrea suddenly so desperate to be student council president? Everyone knew that I was the one really interested in politics. It wasn't fair that she just jumped in and tried to ruin all my dreams.

Someone slapped me on the back. I turned to see Christopher Poole grinning at me. "I hear Badger's looking for you, your most high kingliness." He walked away, still grinning.

They were all out to get me.

I sat on one of the stone benches facing the school doors so that Badger couldn't sneak up on me. I bit into the meat loaf sandwich Dad had made, suddenly feeling sick at the sight of the catsup that oozed out around the bread.

"Uh-oh," someone said.

The chatter in the courtyard stopped. I looked up to see Badger stomping toward me. I scrambled to my feet, holding the sandwich up like a shield.

Badger looked down into my face. "We're going to have one of those fights that they had back in those old days. Like a duel. One of those, um . . ."

Willie Fisher had rushed into the courtyard behind Badger. He moved to stand beside me. "It's a joust, you oaf. If you're challenging the king, it's my job as his knight to fight for him on the field of honor."

I looked around at the growing crowd. If I let Willie fight my battle, my political career would die before it even got started.

"Thanks, Willie, but no thanks. Okay, Badger, you're on. We'll joust this Saturday at Craven's Field," I said.

"And winner is king for the rest of the project," Badger added.

Andrea squealed. "What? No way am I queen with a Badger king. It's bad enough with Justin."

Badger laughed at her.

"How do you decide who the winner is?" Carlos asked.

I glared at him. He and Lester should have been standing beside me, three friends against one bully. Instead, they were part of the crowd, waiting to see if Badger was going to dethrone me. They had promised to support me when I signed up to run for fifth-grade president. I didn't expect it to be so lonely at the top.

Willie moved closer and whispered, "Stand tall against your enemies, King Justin."

Badger grinned. "The winner is the one who can walk away."

I didn't like the look in Badger's eye. "Let's just say the one who hits the ground first loses. We need a referee."

"I'll do it," Willie shouted.

"Yeah, right. You're his knight."

Willie frowned. "That may be so, but I'm always fair. I will be impartial."

"All right." Badger pointed at me and announced. "Bikes and armor. Nine o'clock Saturday morning. Graven's Field. And be ready to turn over your crown . . . and your teeth."

He whirled around and stomped out of the courtyard.

Willie tugged at my sleeve. "Your Majesty—um, Justin, that was very brave."

I groaned. "And very stupid."

Willie walked away, shaking his head. I stared after him and wondered how many kings fired their own knights.

Andrea stood in front of me. "You'd better not lose. I refuse to be queen with Badger as king. Besides, I'd win this election easy if you lose and I want to prove I'm the best girl for the job." She left the courtyard with her ladies-in-waiting, passing out flyers as she went.

I sat down to finish my sandwich. Every condemned man got to have a last meal.

Chapter 12

♕

Bribing the Kingdom

Future Politician's Rule #12—A slice of pizza for every voter.

It wasn't easy to keep my mind on campaigning while visions of Badger jousting me off my throne rattled my brain. But it was only two weeks until Election Day and I had to concentrate on winning over the fifth-grade voters.

Thursday after school I took the phone to my room and began working on my campaign promises.

"Joe's Pizza Parlor."

I cleared my throat and talked as deep as I could. "Hello, sir. I'm the food manager at Payton Intermediate School and we'd like to sample your pizzas for our Pizza Party Fridays."

"Sample our pizzas?" the voice asked.

I nodded. "Yes, a taste test for our students. If you could deliver twenty-five pizzas to the school cafeteria tomorrow at precisely 11:20, we'll have our expert tasters sample them."

"Is this some kind of prank?"

"Oh no, sir," I squeaked, then lowered my voice again. "Just think of the business you'll get. Pizzas delivered every Friday for the rest of the year."

I heard several voices whispering to one another. "Hmmm, interesting. Who'll pay for the pizzas we bring tomorrow?"

I had a feeling Mrs. Winthrop would hit the roof if I billed the school. "Do you have an advertising budget?" I asked.

More voices whispering. "Are you asking us to do this for free?"

"Advertising," I repeated. "Think about the long-term benefits your company will get. Just one week of free pizzas to get a school's business from now until the end of May."

"Okay, tell you what. We'll send five medium pizzas with different toppings on each. But if we don't get your business, we charge the school. Deal?"

I held my breath. I'd have to worry about that later if I couldn't convince the PTA to pay. "Make it five large and we're in business," I said.

"Fine. We'll be there tomorrow. Who do we ask for?"

I stared at the phone. "Umm, have the delivery guy slip in the side door and put the pizzas on the nearest table. Tell him that Mr. Davies will meet him there."

I hung up the phone. This would get everyone's attention.

The next morning in gym class I passed the word around about the pizza. This time, I was the first guy chosen for basketball.

I was dribbling down the court, getting ready to pass the ball to Carlos, when there were shouts from the girls' gym. Coach ran out the door. He came back a moment later.

"Davies, come with me."

Lester gave me a push. "Ooh, you're invited to the girls' gym, Your Majesty."

I shrugged. "When you're king, everyone wants your attention."

I ran behind Coach. We walked into the girls' gym. Mrs. Hawk was chasing behind a high-heeled woman who carried a notepad and a tape measure.

"Ma'am, you will have to leave this gym right now," Mrs. Hawk shouted. "No street shoes in the gym."

The woman stopped beside Marilyn Gray at the uneven bars. Marilyn did a flip over the low bar and landed on the mat in perfect position. The strange woman began measuring Marilyn's waist.

"What's going on?" I asked Coach.

He turned to me and scowled. "I was about to ask you the same thing. Is this another of your disruptions?"

I shook my head. I was being blamed for everything. "No, sir. Honest."

Mrs. Hawk grabbed the woman by the arm and walked her over to where Coach and I stood.

"Justin, if this is your idea of . . ."

Andrea ran across the room. "Mrs. Hawk, Justin isn't the only fifth grader who wants to help his classmates." She pointed to the wide-eyed woman being held prisoner by Mrs. Hawk. "This is my mother's tailor, Ms. Cecilia Ducharme. She is here to measure us for better fitting gym suits."

I grinned at Andrea. I had to admit, she was as sneaky as me.

Mrs. Hawk threw her hands in the air. "Andrea Carey, you have caused a huge disturbance in my class. There will be no new gym suits, tailored or otherwise."

Andrea frowned. I knew how she felt. But I was glad her plan hadn't worked. Coach apologized for blaming me while we walked back to gym.

One loss for Andrea. And I still had pizza to win over the voters.

Even before the lunch bell rang, I could smell the warm pizzas from Mr. Bailey's classroom. The guys grinned and nudged one another.

Even Mr. Bailey smiled. "That doesn't smell like our usual cafeteria cuisine." He glanced at me when I high-fived Lester. "Is there something you'd like to tell me about, Justin?"

I shook my head. "No, sir, but you might want to go to the cafeteria instead of the teachers' lounge today."

The moment the bell rang I hopped out of my chair and ran out the door. Willie was right behind me.

"Justin, as your knight and campaign manager, I would like to know what you are up to," Willie said, moving to stand in front of me.

I stopped and shook my head. "I'm trying to keep my promises and gain everyone's vote," I said. "If you want pizza, you'd better get to the cafeteria before it's gone."

Willie's eyebrows rose. "You ordered pizza for the whole school?"

I shook my head. "No, just a little sampling." I pushed past him and hurried down A Hall.

There was a lot of noise coming from the cafeteria.

I walked inside and was knocked down.

"Sorry, Your Majesty," someone shouted as he ran past.

Willie walked in and stared down at me.

"This is just what I was afraid would happen, King Justin. If there isn't enough pizza for everyone, they'll turn into a mob."

I got up off the floor and stared at the chaos. A wide-eyed pizza delivery guy stood behind a table where rows of kids pushed and shoved to grab slices of pizza. The floor was slippery with smeared cheese and tomato sauce.

The cafeteria ladies were banging ladles against pots and shouting at the crowd. Trash overflowed with lunch sacks and trays of cafeteria food that kids had abandoned.

"Uh-oh," Willie said.

Mrs. Winthrop walked toward us. My mouth dropped when her foot slipped on a piece of pizza, and she spilled to the floor.

"Justin Davies!"

I took a deep breath and went to the office to wait for her.

Chapter 13

♛

Practice Makes Almost Perfect

Future Politician's Rule #13—
Hire a double!

I had after-school detention for the pizza pandemonium, but Willie had waited for me and invited me over to practice jousting. My pizza plan hadn't worked so well, so I was ready to let Willie help me with the joust. I couldn't depend on Lester and Carlos who both said they were busy. Wasn't there a way to rule the fifth grade and still have my best friends?

"Take this," Willie said, shoving a cardboard box across the floor of his garage.

I struggled to carry the box into Willie's backyard.

Willie unpacked it and shoved an odd assortment of things into my hands.

"I've been reading up on jousting. It was used for entertainment at festivals, but there were quite a few injuries," Willie explained. "So, the first thing is to outfit you for safety."

I nodded. "Sounds like a great idea to me. Wrap me in a rubber suit and I'll just bounce when Badger knocks me off my bike in two seconds flat."

Willie frowned. "You're not thinking positively."

I waved the football helmet in my hand. "Well, I'm positive that my kingly behind is going to be smeared all over the ground."

Willie grabbed three pillows from a bag and began fluffing them one at a time. He put them against his chest as if testing them. "Justin, Your Majesty, why don't you listen to my ideas. After all, I may be the first kid to stand up to Badger and survive with my face intact."

"That's because I jumped in and distracted him," I said.

Willie smiled. "Of course, that's what best friends are for. Now, let me return the favor and help you practice for Sunday." He picked up my bike. "We should practice at the school. My driveway's not long enough."

I folded my arms and glared at Willie. It was his fault I was in this mess in the first place. But there was no point getting worked up about that now. If I didn't win the joust, Badger might convince Mr. Bailey to let him take over as king. Even if he didn't, even if Mr. Bailey got mad about the joust and stopped the project, I would be the loser in everyone's eyes. I needed another me—one for the joust, one for campaigning.

"Okay, let's go for it," I said.

I refused to practice with the costume on. I didn't want anyone to see me in that outfit until there was no other choice. Besides, it was hard enough just practicing holding the pool cue Willie had borrowed from his dad.

"We won't be able to use this for the actual joust," Willie explained. "Besides, it's too dangerous. I'll find something else."

After I'd ridden back and forth across the parking lot nine times and crashed seven of them, I could barely walk straight.

"Okay, that's enough practicing. Let's get you into shape," Willie said.

I groaned. "You just knocked me out of any shape I had."

Five minutes later Willie was riding my bicycle, and I was running behind him. He wasn't very good at riding straight, but he could pedal fast.

"Come on, Your Majesty, keep up," Willie ordered. "While you're running, I'll share some of my favorite quotes from our great leaders."

He chattered away as I huffed and puffed

until I was sure I'd lose my political cookies all over the sidewalk. The rest of the afternoon, I practiced on the bike, jogged, and did push-ups to build up my arm muscles.

"Enough," I said, dropping into the nearest patch of grass. "I'll abdicate the throne right now unless we quit. I need a soda and piles of junk food." I sat up and winced.

We walked to the Stop & Shop for some sugar and carbs. Willie inhaled his cupcake and drink. By the time we got back to his house, I'd finished mine, too.

We put my jousting outfit into a box.

"Well, guess I'd better get back home," I said.

Willie grabbed my bike handlebar. "Wait, I wanted to talk with you about some ideas for your student council campaign."

I leaned on my bike. I could use all the help I could get, thanks to Andrea.

"Okay, I'll listen."

I followed Willie into the house and upstairs to his room. I imagined how perfectly neat it would be. And boring.

"Wow!"

I stood in the doorway to Willie's room and looked around. It was almost as messy as mine—clothes piled on the bed, an overflowing trash can, schoolbooks tossed on a chair, magazines and books stacked on a shaky-looking bookcase.

But best of all, there were pictures of presidents all around the room. One wall had laminated posters of the Declaration of Independence, the Pledge of Allegiance, and a chart showing the political tree from a local city councilman up to the president and his cabinet.

"You're that interested in politics?" I asked.

Willie nodded. "It's my own private little dream. Actually, I'm not the leader type, as you probably know, but I would do well as a private secretary to a politician or perhaps a close personal friend and confidant who shares great plans and ideas."

Willie picked up a scrapbook on his desk. Inside were pictures of men I'd never seen before.

"These are the men who formed the presidential cabinets of some of our great presidents," Willie explained. He pointed to a fuzzy photo of a man shaking the hand of President John F. Kennedy. "This was Kennedy's secretary of agriculture, Orville Freeman. Now, with a name like Orville he must have been teased in school. It's one of those names like . . . like Willie."

I shrugged. "So, he had a funny name."

"It's not the name, it's the job. How many people can name all the secretaries of agriculture or postmasters general? But these were the men who helped the president in hard times. They were the men who advised him and gave him strength when he was wearing down from the pressures. They stuck by him."

I stared at Willie. He closed the scrapbook and set it back on his desk. Yes, I could imagine Willie as the man behind the man . . . a little bulldozer pushing people into situations they'd never agree to on their own.

I cleared my throat. "Um, okay. Really cool, Willie. So, what are these great ideas you have?"

Willie ran over to a desk in the corner of his room. It was the one clean spot in the room. There was nothing on it but a computer and printer. Willie grabbed a piece of paper from the printer.

"Don't be upset, Justin, but I think you and Andrea are going about your campaigns all wrong," he said.

I folded my arms. "Oh yeah?"

Willie nodded. He shook the piece of paper in my face. "Just listen to all the things you both have promised so far. Ice cream in the cafeteria, a pool, Test-free Mondays . . . every week, phones in lockers, lighted mirrors in the bathroom . . . and there's a lot more. You promised Gary Hinkens that he'd pass fifth grade this year. You can't keep that promise. No one can."

I frowned. "Well, maybe I've gotten a little carried away, but everyone expects the candidates to make promises."

Willie's eyes went wide as he pointed to the

list. "But, Your Majesty . . . Justin . . . you even promised that you'd *keep* all your promises."

It's true. I had promised to keep my promises at the PTA meeting, in the hallways, in Mr. Bailey's room, and the cafeteria. I even wrote it down on a piece of paper and stuck it on my locker door.

Willie stared at me. I shrugged. "They'll forget all that when I'm student council president."

Willie shook his head. "I don't think so. But what if you make one or two big promises and find a way to get it done?"

One promise? What president won the election on just one promise? Or even two?

"No way, Willie, Andrea's got Priscilla's rich daddy to help her out. She's making lots of promises and I have to keep up."

"I hope you know what you are doing." Willie crumpled the list into a ball and tossed it at his trash can. It landed a foot away. "But now that you're about to show the voters that bullies like Badger can't win, you are sure to convince everyone you are the true king of fifth grade."

I groaned. For a second, I'd forgotten about the joust. "Badger is going to cream me."

Willie ignored me. "It's an honor to be your knight. What a kingdom you and I will build."

If this was building a kingdom, I didn't think I'd survive the construction.

Chapter 14

♕

Joust a Minute!

Future Politician's Rule #14—
Never bleed on your constituents.

Early Saturday morning, I slipped out to meet Willie at his house. I would change into my jousting outfit in Willie's garage.

Carlos and Lester were waiting for me on Willie's front porch. I was shocked.

"What are you guys doing here?" I asked. They hadn't done one thing to help me as king if it wasn't fun for them, and definitely nothing to help me win the election. I didn't know whether to tell them to go home or pretend we were friends again.

Carlos jabbed Lester with his elbow. "Badger as king isn't my idea of a class project. It would be a disaster. It would be like the Joker guarding for Batman's basketball team."

Lester nodded. We followed Willie into his garage. Lester and Carlos watched solemnly as he prepared my outfit, piece by piece.

"There. All done," Willie said. He stood back and looked me up and down.

I walked across the garage to a full-length mirror that had been propped against a wall. I slid my feet across the room like the Frankenstein monster. Riding my bike in this costume would be impossible.

As I stared at the mirrored reflection, I had to admit that Willie had thought of everything. He'd even given me a football helmet as a knight's helmet and visor. Willie had painted a large green *J* on it.

"Green is the perfect color," I said. "It'll match my face."

Willie tied the pillows onto my chest and back with jump rope. The plastic ends dangled against my shoulders like a pair of deflated wings. I raised my arms and legs. The cotton balls stuffed inside my shirtsleeves and pants legs were beginning to itch.

"Now," Willie said. "The last thing you'll put on before the joust begins is this catcher's mask to doubly protect your face."

"Huh?" I asked, tapping the helmet. Willie's voice sounded muffled. I took off the helmet.

"No way. Who do you think I am, JELL-O Man? I'm covered head to toe already. Enough."

Lester hopped around me, punching the pillow and cushioned arms. "Wow, I bet old Badger didn't think of all this padding. Hey, what do you call a king who's lost his stuffing? A giant dead turkey."

"Thanks for the vote of confidence," I said, trying to walk across the room without falling over. "Badger's got plenty of his own padding."

"Let's get moving!" Willie ordered. He pushed my bike out of the garage.

Carlos, Lester, and I followed behind.

Carlos spoke without looking at me. "You scared?"

I tried to fold my arms, but the cotton made it impossible. "Me? No way! Well . . . maybe a little."

We turned the corner to Craven's Field.

"Wow! Look at that crowd," Willie shouted. "It's perfect publicity, Justin."

"Yeah, I'll be publicly smashed, trashed, and dethroned," I said.

Badger walked across the parking lot, looking like a spaceman. He wore a plastic helmet that had a breathing hole for the mouth. A cardboard shield hung over his chest, covered in foil. More foil had been wrapped around his arms, legs, and waist.

"You look like a marshmallow that grew a

really ugly head," Badger said, rolling his black-and-gold Schwinn beside him.

"What kind of outfit is that supposed to be?" I asked, pointing to Badger's costume. "This isn't a weenie roast. Or maybe it is."

"I'm the Silver Knight." Badger moved toward me.

Carlos gave Badger a thumbs-up. "Hey, we're just wondering where we could get one."

Carlos and Lester walked away to join the other peasants.

Willie cleared his throat. He pulled two bathroom plungers from a sack. "I've brought your lances."

Just what Badger needed, a stick for marshmallow roasting.

I turned to the waiting crowd. "Wouldn't you rather see a debate? Or perhaps a brutal game of chess?"

"No!" Everyone yelled. "Joust. Joust. JOUST!"

Standing in front of the crowd was the little second-grade kid I'd seen Badger leading to the bus. He shouted, "Go Badger!" Poor kid, he'd been brainwashed.

Willie patted my shoulder. "Fine speech. But you promised a battle."

Priscilla blew a whistle and shouted, "Queen Andrea would like to say a word now."

I groaned.

Andrea held a cheerleader megaphone to

her mouth. "Boys use violence to solve their problems. Vote for the peaceful candidate. Me!"

"No peace, we want a joust!" someone shouted from the crowd.

Andrea pointed the megaphone at me. "I hope you both get your blocks knocked off. Then we'll see who's in charge around here."

Willie grabbed the megaphone from Andrea's hand and shouted, "The jousters will begin at those two trees with red ribbons tied around them." Willie pointed to the edges of the field. "Badger at the far tree, Justin, the nearest."

The trees were about fifty feet apart and a long stretch of wide yellow tape lay on the ground between them.

"When Andrea gives the word, you will ride toward each other, poles extended," Willie continued. "Your objective will be to knock the other from his bike. There will be three passes. If you are both upright by the third pass, the joust will be declared a tie and you will, uh . . . co-reign as dual kings."

"Uh-uh," Badger said. "I'm a one-man team."

"You mean one-gorilla," Lester mumbled.

Willie rubbed his hands together. "Let's get this over with."

I could think of lots of places I'd rather be. Stuck at the top of a roller coaster. Being force-fed Dad's meat loaf. Even cleaning out the school toilets with a toothbrush.

I walked my bike past the crowd, stopping where Andrea and Priscilla stood. Andrea, no longer in costume, wore a pair of black jeans, a red T-shirt, and a purple scarf around her neck.

"Andrea . . . as my queen," I whispered so no one would hear, "if I survive the joust, you will of course shout hysterically how proud you are of me."

She looked at me the same way Mom looks at dead cockroaches. "Get real," she said.

Shot down again, by my own queen.

I turned and fled to my bicycle—well, not *fled*, really, but I moved as fast as Sir Frankenpillow could move.

Willie ran beside me yammering instructions.

"Don't look like you're afraid, your future voters are watching."

When we reached the tree at the farthest end of the yellow stripe, I took a deep breath and patted the handlebars of my seven-year-old bike with its chipped blue paint. "Come on, trusty steed."

Willie held out the plunger. "Here is your royal plunger . . . I mean . . . lance."

Andrea walked to the middle of the parking lot, raised a red scarf, and dropped it to the ground.

With a lot of pushing from Willie, I finally was on my bike. I gasped for air and yelled, "Charge!"

Chapter 15

♕

And the Crown Belongs to . . .

Future Politician's Rule #15—When all else fails, charge ahead!

Closer and closer I ride toward Badger.
I'm heading straight for him.
I'm going to knock his block off.
I'm going to leave here as a triumphant king.
I . . .
I . . . missed him.
He missed me!
I looked back and saw my own surprise mirrored by the disbelieving look on Badger's face.
"Aaagh!" I yelled as my bike hit a bump and skidded. I bounced off the bike and onto the cement. At least the pillows worked.

I sat up and saw Badger sprawled across his bike.

"Hey, that doesn't count, does it?" I yelled.

Willie frowned, then shook his head. "No, I suppose not. That will be your trial run. But no more goofing off."

Two kids ran from the crowd to help me to my feet. I glanced over at Carlos and Lester who were laughing.

I mounted my steed again. Half my cotton was lying on the ground. At least it was easier to move my arms.

"Go!" Andrea screamed.

The bicycle wobbled beneath me as I struggled to keep my lance from falling off the handlebars. The faster I pedaled, the more I wobbled.

Like a train barreling at full speed, Badger rode straight toward me. I took one hand off the handlebars to grab for my plunger. The bike weaved and I fought for control.

The sun moved from behind a cloud, glinting off Badger's silver-foil outfit.

Our bikes passed and I swung my lance wildly. It hit the handlebars on Badger's bike.

Badger's plunger grazed my shoulder. I glanced back, feeling a moment of triumph when Badger teetered as if about to lose his balance. Then, the moment vanished. Badger dropped his plunger and slowed his bike.

"Rats!" I said.

The crowd booed and hissed. "Knock his block off, Justin!"

"Kick the king's royal behind!"

I rode to the fence and stopped. I stared at the crowd and saw Austin Burrison with a video camera. Great, someday I'll have a movie to show my kids of the biggest defeat of my life. I stepped off my bike.

Andrea gave Badger the pole and walked back to the center. "Go!" she shouted again.

Go? Was she kidding? I wasn't even on my bike yet. Even after losing some of the cotton, sitting on my bike seat was still like balancing a grapefruit on the tip of a pencil.

This time, David Murphy, Richard Andrews, *and* Willie had to help get me back on my bike. I was glad when I saw two big guys pushing Badger on his bike. We were both overweighted and tired.

"Will you two get going?" Andrea yelled. "I have a campaign meeting in an hour."

My feet hit the pedals and I was headed for glory or a gory mess.

"Aaargh!" Badger yelled as we met. My lance missed him and his bike by a foot.

"Oof!" I said as the suction end of Badger's lance made contact with my stomach. The lance bounced off the pillow tied to my chest. I laughed.

I dropped my plunger and turned to wave at my subjects. My bike did a dance. It wobbled and weaved, shimmied and shook. The crowd gasped. Willie yelled, "No!"

But I twisted the handlebars sharply to the left and got control of the bike once more. I rode to my starting point and stopped. My breath came in gasps.

"One more time," Willie shouted. "Good luck, Your Majesty."

Badger pointed his plunger at Willie. "When I'm king, Wimpy Willie, you'll be shining my armor with your tongue!"

I cringed. Badger didn't look the least bit tired now. Somehow, he'd gotten a second wind. In fact, he grinned at me and began doing bicep curls with his lance.

"Yield now and you can be my royal footrest," Badger yelled.

I slammed my hands on the bars of my bicycle.

"The king does not yield! I'm ready," I proclaimed.

Andrea gave the signal one more time. I glared at Badger. "This school's about to lose one bully," I whispered.

I grasped my lance. This time, I pedaled at a steady pace, keeping my eyes on Badger's lance.

Badger raised his plunger and swung as if he were playing baseball with my head as the ball.

"Watch out!" Willie yelled.

Andrea screamed.

I ducked.

Our bikes smashed together, the handle-bars catching.

"Get away!" Badger shouted, sticking the plunger onto the top of my football helmet. Our bicycles tottered as he pushed. Badger bellowed and threw up his hands.

Half bent over the back end of Badger's bike, I swung my plunger back, catching Badger on his backside. The plunger stuck fast, wobbling like a tail.

Badger did a somersault onto the ground, pulling me down with him.

We rolled around, reaching for our lances to do plunger-to-plunger battle.

"Get off me!" Badger yelled.

"No, not until you yield," I said. "Say, 'I'm a two-headed, rotten-smelling troll.' Say it."

Badger shoved me away at the same time, reaching around as he did to pull the plunger from his backside with a *plop*.

"Stop!" Willie shouted. "The joust is over."

I rolled on the ground, struggling to untie the pillows. "We both fell off our bikes, so it's a tie."

Badger kicked one of the pillows. "If it's a tie, I'll just pound you now, and then I'm king."

Austin ran toward us with the camcorder. The crowd of kids parted, whispering. I could almost see them placing bets.

Willie grabbed the camcorder from Austin's

hand. "Excuse me, but this is royal business! We can review the tape, Your Majesty, and see who hit the ground first."

Everyone waited as the tape was rewound.

Badger, Willie, and I crowded around the camcorder to watch.

"Look, I hit you first," I said.

Badger snorted. "See how your bike is going out of control? It's your fault we got tangled."

We moved closer as the tiny screen showed Badger flip over his bike and pull me with him. Badger landed face first on the ground, with me falling on top of him.

"You hit the ground first," I said, tapping the tiny screen.

"Long live King Justin!" Willie shouted.

I imagined "Hail to the Chief" playing in the distance. Applause, whistles, and a few boos came from the crowd. Andrea ran to my side.

Taking a deep breath, I turned to wave at the other kids. My people. I had won my first big battle for leadership. Being king wasn't so hard.

I nudged Andrea. "Tell everyone how great I am. And then you can drop out of the race for student council president."

Andrea shook her head and whispered out of the side of her mouth. "You may be king of Mr. Bailey's project, but I'm going to be fifth-grade president."

She turned and gave the crowd a big smile.

"In honor of Justin's win, Priscilla and I will host a doughnut and hot chocolate breakfast Monday morning before school. And, remember, vote for Andrea Carey for fifth-grade president, the candidate who fights *for* you, not *with* you."

My jaw dropped. The crowd cheered.

Andrea curtsied to the crowd. She and Priscilla walked across the field and got into a big black sedan.

"Woohoo! You're still king," Carlos said, slapping me on the back. "I'll take the best of two evils."

"What does that mean?" I asked.

Carlos glanced at Lester. Neither one of them answered.

Willie glowered at them before shaking his finger at me. "Yes, you've kept your title, Justin, but you gave us a scare. Next time, perhaps you'd better put in some more practice."

I turned to bid farewell to my followers, but the field had cleared.

"Where'd they all go?"

Lester shrugged. "It's Saturday morning. We've got better stuff to do than listen to one of your speeches."

I watched Lester and Carlos leave, took off my "armor," and shoved it into Willie's hands.

Willie staggered. "Your Majesty, now that your crown is safe, shouldn't we concentrate on your campaign?"

I groaned. "Willie, I know what I'm doing. If I don't make promises, I don't get votes. If I don't get votes, I don't win. If Andrea wins, I'm changing my name and moving to Australia to live with kangaroos."

No. I didn't need a backup plan. It was time to forge ahead and keep to my ideas. Nothing could stop me now. Long live the king!

Chapter 16

♔

Invitation to a Feast

Future Politician's Rule #16—
Always influence the influential.

I strolled onto the school grounds Monday morning and was greeted with applause. No cheers, though. Everyone was stuffing their faces with Andrea's free doughnuts.

I shook hands with the kids hanging around the front of the school. "Thank you, peasants. Vote for me as student council president," I said, holding my head high. "With me as your president, your problems will disappear. I am prepared to inspire you with one of my speeches . . ."

The crowd disappeared, leaving the front of the school quiet as a ghost town.

Greg Gibbs walked past. "Way to go, Your

Royal-Bag-Of-Wind. If you want to make everyone really happy, promise them no more speeches."

I went to my locker and put my backpack inside. Andrea's locker was three away from mine. A sheet of paper was taped to the door.

WHAT DO YOU NEED FROM YOUR NEXT STUDENT COUNCIL PRESIDENT? LET ME KNOW! I'M HERE FOR YOU!

There were twelve lines filled. Some of the suggestions weren't bad, such as having a waitress in the cafeteria, a class field trip to Space Center Houston complete with astronaut autographs, and personal CD players in every classroom. Others were a little scary, like the request for Andrea to banish a certain king back to elementary school forever.

How was I going to compete with Andrea's campaign promises? Everywhere I turned there was a flyer on the wall about voting for Andrea. She and her giggly friends were like little tornadoes. My friends were full of hot air. They were too busy playing court jesters and getting mad every time I did something they didn't like to help me with my own campaign.

Willie had been my only real ally in my plan to become fifth-grade president. He was Sam to my Frodo. Robin to my Batman.

But was he my friend? Did I have friends anymore, or just voters?

I hurried to PE. My locker was crammed with rolls of toilet paper. At least this time, I had taken my gym clothes home over the weekend. I changed clothes and hurried into the gym. The coach was setting up the horse, my favorite part of gymnastics. I tried to ignore the duct tape covering the top and sides of the dying horse as I prepared to leap this mighty steed.

Then I saw Badger. He stood off to himself, pounding his fist into his palm. Okay, so not everyone loved their king.

Badger snarled at me every time we passed each other. Coach Friedman finally made him sit on the bleachers after he tripped me when I was running toward the horse. Everyone else patted me on the back and congratulated me for the joust . . . once Badger was on the other side of the gym.

"I'm moving up," I told Carlos and Lester after class as we showered and dressed. I was determined to pretend they weren't ignoring me. "Some of these kids have influential parents—important people on the school board or in the community."

"Hey," Carlos said. "Aren't *we* important people?"

I pulled a ruler from my math book. I touched each of my friends' shoulders. "The most important. You're the first court jesters to be knighted. 'Course, it's unofficial."

Lester shook his head. "Either we're official or we're out of here."

We just stared at one another. "It's Mr. Bailey's rules," I said.

They walked out of the locker room and slammed the door.

Willie came over to me, spraying deodorant wildly.

"Enough," I said, gagging.

We were the last ones to leave. Willie and I walked down the hall toward history class.

"Hey!" a voice yelled.

I looked up to see Badger walking toward us. It was becoming a habit, seeing that snarling face coming at me.

"You just wait until you're not king anymore. You'll just be Justin Davies, a guy waiting to have his face rearranged by my fist." He shook his red notebook in my face.

I leaned into his face. "Listen here, you over-grown cliché . . ."

"What did you call me?" Badger yelled.

"A cliché. You act like some cardboard bully with no personality. Everyone has something good about them. I bet you could be a nice guy if you tried. I bet you're smarter than you act, too. Instead of threatening everyone, why don't you spend some time finding what's good about you?"

Badger blinked. "I . . . uh . . . well . . . um . . ." He scratched his head and looked around, then turned and walked away.

"Very impressive," Willie said. "One of your lectures finally left him speechless."

I grinned at my knight. The second period tardy bell rang and we ran to history class.

"Thanks for showing up, boys," Mr. Bailey said as Willie flung open the classroom door.

"Sorry," I said. "We were taking care of king's business."

I slipped into my seat and opened my history book. I tried to pay attention, but I couldn't.

Mr. Bailey passed out last week's history test, then sat on the corner of his desk.

"Well, class, this is the beginning of your second and last week to have a king and queen. I hope you're taking lots of notes for your essay. It will be a big part of your grade this semester."

Carlos raised his hand.

"Yes?" Mr. Bailey asked.

"Does Badger flunk for being wiped out at the joust?"

Badger growled from the dungeon. Mr. Bailey shook his head. "First of all, that joust wasn't part of the project. If I'd have known about it beforehand, it would have been canceled. Second, I'd advise you to worry about your own grade, Carlos."

Mr. Bailey held a piece of paper that he unrolled like a scroll. Clearing his throat, he read, "Hear ye, hear ye, all citizens of the Kingdom of Bailey. On Wednesday night at half past six bells, there will be a royal banquet in the cafeteria, in honor of His and Her Majesties, King Justin and Queen Andrea."

The classroom erupted in applause and whistles.

"A party!" Lester yelled. "It's about time."

"There will be much music, merriment, and feasting for everyone. All may enter who hold the king or queen's scroll of invitation," Mr. Bailey finished reading.

Mr. Bailey held up a box of small yellow rolls of paper. "Justin and Andrea will each get a box of these. They each have ten scrolls. Not everyone in the kingdom would have been invited to the king's feast. The royal court would have chosen their guests. There are enough invitations for everyone in class. However, it's up to your king and queen who they decide to invite."

"All right!"

"Party!"

I clutched the box that Mr. Bailey placed in my hand. This was my chance to influence those who could best help me win the election.

After class, Andrea and I were surrounded by kids asking for scrolls. It didn't take long for word to spread, and soon kids I barely knew were begging for invitations. Some were in sixth grade. Others were in Mrs. Peterson's history class, and they weren't even doing this project.

"C'mon, I'll wash your dog or bike or parents' car for a month."

"Big deal, *I'll* buy your lunch every day for two weeks!"

"I'll invite you to my next birthday party. It's going to be a cool one, too. My parents are taking us to the Shore Creek Amusement Park."

"I will *not* accept bribes," I informed the crowd.

Andrea shoved me out of the way. "Maybe he won't, but I will. Give me your best offers."

I whispered, "Just don't give one to Badger."

Andrea nodded. "Who do you think I am, the village idiot?"

I wasn't going to answer that question.

As the crowd closed in around Andrea, I slipped away. I shifted the books under one arm while struggling to hold the scrolls in my hands.

"Wow, did you see those poor saps begging for scrolls?" Carlos said, grabbing my books. "Here, buddy, I'll carry these."

Lester nodded. "Yeah, who do they think they are anyway?" He swung his lunch sack in my face. "My mom packed a big piece of chocolate cake with fudge icing. Want it?"

I shook my head and stuffed the scrolls inside my pockets. "Nah, thanks anyway."

"Don't let those peasants bug you," Carlos said. "We know who'll get the first two scrolls."

I took a deep breath. "Look, I know you've been mad at me about choosing Willie as my knight. But you guys are my best friends, so please understand . . . um . . . I can't back down on my plans now. Course, I have to give the first one to Willie. Andrea's giving one to Priscilla. Both our knights should be there. It's important to choose the right people."

Carlos frowned. "I guess so," he mumbled. "But the next two are the most important invitations."

I snapped my fingers. "You're right. I've got to make sure I invite Brett Chapman and Debbie Deur."

"Who?" Carlos and Lester screamed.

Lester dropped the cafeteria rolls he'd been juggling. "They're not even in Mr. Bailey's class."

"Brett's mother and Debbie's father are both on the school board. I'll work up a speech about the boys' gym equipment," I quickly explained. "That only leaves seven tickets. Who else has parents on the board? And I should find out which kids have parents who are important in the business community."

Carlos threw my books on the floor. "What about us?"

"We're your best friends!" Lester said.

"Look, guys," I said. "Friendship has nothing to do with it. I haven't got much time left to keep my promises. Promises I want to make good. I'm doing this for you, the common people, my supporters."

Lester leaned closer. "If you don't invite us, you can add two more common people's names to your list of enemies, right beside Badger's."

I chewed my lip. "Wait, I got it. I know how you can come to the feast."

"Well, that's more like it," Carlos said.

"There's got to be entertainment. You guys can come and do your court jester stuff and entertain the guests," I said.

Carlos and Lester looked at each other, then at me. "No way," Carlos said. "Either we come as guests or forget it. You're turning your back on the home team."

I took a step back. They didn't understand the game of politics. "I'm really sorry, guys, but I can't waste invitations."

"Waste? So now being around us is a waste?" Carlos mumbled.

I stared at him. I hadn't meant that at all. They were my friends, and I wanted them to understand what I was doing and why I was doing it.

Lester leaned over and whispered to Carlos. Carlos grinned and nodded. "Okay, Justin, we'll be the clowns at your party."

"Yeah, your guests will be entertained . . . don't worry," Lester said.

I watched them a moment. "You promise, no funny business?"

Lester nodded. "If we're not funny, we won't be doing our job."

I smiled. "See, I knew we could come to an agreement. You'll be helping me to help you get a great student council president."

Carlos scooped the books off the floor and shoved them into my hand.

I watched them walk away, nudging each other and laughing.

Chapter 17

♛

Dissension in the Ranks

Future Politician's Rule #17—
Beware of angry voters.

I spent most of the rest of Monday hiding in the bathroom between classes. Once I gave out my last invitation to Sally Robinson, whose mom was on the city council last year, I knew I was in trouble.

Willie was waiting for me after school. "Your Majesty, there are rumors of a plot against your royal person. There are whispers that include yours and Badger's name. It would be a good idea if I walked home with you. You must be protected before your crowning moment at the feast."

I laughed. "Willie, I know you're just trying to help, but you aren't much of a bodyguard against Badger. And what do you mean, 'my crowning moment'?"

Willie pulled a wrinkled sheet of paper from his shirt pocket. "This is the list of your invited guests. They are ten guaranteed votes. You must show them a good time and get them to ask their friends to vote for you."

"Good idea, Willie," I said. "All these kids have parents who are influential in the community. I expect them to pay back the favor of being invited to this party by voting for me and introducing me to their parents. If I got each one of them to promise to ask five people to vote for me, that's sixty more votes."

Willie bowed. "Don't forget about me. I plan to ask a lot more than five."

"Thanks," I said. The only problem was that Willie didn't have that many friends at Payton.

When we walked off the school grounds, a school bus drove past us.

"Hey!" a voice yelled.

I looked up and saw Badger sticking his head out an open window. "I'll get you, King Just-A-Wimp." He pointed to Willie. "And your little dog, too!"

I was glad he was on the bus and not sneaking up behind me.

"You don't need to walk me home," I told Willie.

Willie stuffed the guest list back into his

pocket. "Okay, I'll go home and work on your campaign posters."

He waved good-bye and turned down the next street. Campaign posters? I hadn't even thought about asking Willie to do it. Lester and Carlos were great friends, at least they used to be, but I don't think they would have spent so much time coming up with ways to help me win the election.

I was glad Monday was over and no one would be bugging me for invitations to the feast.

But Tuesday was worse. By then, everyone knew who had been given an invitation to the royal banquet. Andrea invited all girls, except for Sam Gam, a new guy with a weird name who looked like a kid movie star.

When I walked into English class at the end of the day, my desk was piled with notes. Some were bribes, begging me to sneak them in to the banquet. Others were threats. Badger just kept shaking his fist at me whenever I looked toward the dungeon.

Elaine Goodson and Roger Brooks stopped me in the hall after school.

I slammed my locker shut. "Look, I'm sorry, but there are no more invitations to the feast."

Roger shrugged. "I have choir practice that night. What I want to know is, where's the ice-cream machine you promised for the cafeteria?"

Elaine stepped between us. "Forget ice cream. I want to know when we're going to have homework-free weekends? Have you talked to the fifth-grade teachers? I have lots of things planned for next weekend, and I don't want any homework getting in the way."

I stared at them. I remembered promising the ice-cream machine, and I wasn't about to tell Roger that Mrs. Winthrop had turned down every vendor I'd sent to her office. But I didn't remember promising anyone they wouldn't have homework on the weekends. There was no way teachers were going for that one. The best I was hoping for was test-free Mondays.

Where was Willie when I needed him? I needed an excuse. One that could buy me more time. One that was believable.

"I think I have malaria. I need to go home."

I ran past them and out the door. Someone shouted my name, but I just kept running. As I turned the corner on my street, I saw just how upset someone had been about not getting invited to the banquet. Or was it because of an unkept promise I'd made?

All over the trees in the front lawn, toilet paper hung like Christmas lights. Someone must have skipped last period to get here so fast.

A note on the front door read: "To the king, here's something for your throne." I thought it must have been Badger, but the handwriting wasn't his. It looked more like Lester's. And it sounded like one of his corny jokes. Then I found a math book lying under a bush. Inside the cover was scribbled, "Badger the Bad." And underneath it, a book about basketball legends.

Badger, Carlos, and Lester together? T.P.ing my yard? It couldn't be true.

I spent an hour cleaning up the mess.

That night I dreamed that I was sitting on a throne outside the school. There was a line of kids all around the block waiting to ask favors. I promised each person that I'd make his or her dreams come true. Willie stood beside me in a rusty knight's costume and wrote down each promised favor. He gave the list to a dragon who had Mrs. Winthrop's curly hair. The dragon burned the list to ashes. Then Badger, Lester, and Carlos T.P.ed me and my throne.

Wednesday morning I was half asleep when I stumbled into gym class.

Coach Friedman ordered us to line up. "We're going to have a good old-fashioned game of dodgeball. Number off one and two and split into teams."

I mumbled "two" when my turn came. We were first to line up against the wall. Willie was on my team. So was Badger. At least he wouldn't be hurling balls at me. He kept dodging into me, though.

"Cut it out," I said. "We haven't started yet."

Badger grinned and walked to the other side of the line.

"Remember, aim for the feet," Coach said. "Spread out."

He handed out three balls to the opposing team. I stared into their faces. They were all staring at me. Carlos and Lester, Christopher Poole, Roger Brooks, and a half dozen guys I'd thrown into the dungeon.

The first ball came at me like a cannonball. I dodged to the left and it hit the wall beside me. Another ball hurtled to my left. I moved to my right this time. Two more balls pounded the wall beside me. The rest of the guys against the wall just stood around and watched me do all the dodging.

I glanced toward Coach for help, but he was talking to Mrs. Hawk and had his back to me.

"Hey, guys, no fair," I said. "There's a lot more targets here than just me."

Roger grabbed a ball from Lester's hand. "Oh, sorry, I promise not to try to hit you, Your Majesty." His ball missed my knee by inches. "Oops, guess I forgot to keep my promise."

I folded my arms and stood straight against the wall. "Go ahead, assassinate your king and you're left with Andrea as ruler."

The balls stopped. I smirked. I knew they'd come to their senses.

Carlos, Christopher, and Roger each grabbed a ball and stood together. Lester said, "One, two, three!"

My mouth dropped as the balls flew toward me all at once. Suddenly, Willie screamed, "No-o-o-o! I'll save you!" He leaped in front of me, arms stretched wide. The balls pounded his feet and legs. Willie hit the floor with a loud "Ooof."

I bent down beside him. "Willie, Willie! Are you okay? Speak to me!"

Willie sat up and rubbed his ankle. "Just doing my job as your knight and campaign manager."

I shook my head. "Amazing, Willie. You took three dodge balls for me."

Coach Friedman had rushed over at Willie's shout. He helped Willie up, then growled at the rest of us, "Hit the showers. Then I want all of you on the bleachers, and I expect a one-page essay from each of you on 'What It Means to Be a Good Sport.'"

I had a feeling Coach was going to be glad when the history project was over. I didn't think he'd be voting for Mr. Bailey for Teacher of the Year.

As I sat on the hard bleacher writing my essay, I wondered if I was going to get more than two votes. Mine and Willie's.

Chapter 18

♛

Party Thy Royal Self

Future Politician's Rule #18— Always expect the unexpected.

I went home alone again after school. Carlos and Lester said they were practicing their comedy act for the party. I asked them if I could watch, but they said they wanted to surprise me.

I grabbed a brown banana from the fruit bowl and locked the door to my room. I didn't want to be disturbed by anyone while I worked on my list of influential people coming to the feast. If I could just get their parents to help me keep all my promises, I was sure to win the election.

By the time I finished, I had only twenty minutes to dress for the party.

The phone rang and I heard Dad grab the hall phone.

"Hello?" he said.

After a moment, he hung up. "That's odd," he said.

"What?" I called from my room.

Dad walked down the hall and knocked on my door. I opened it just a crack.

"A voice just growled at me and hung up," he said.

"That's weird. Uh, must've been a wrong number," I said, shutting the door quickly.

After I finished dressing, I stuck a notepad in my costume for important information I would get from my important guests.

"How do I look, Dad?" I asked.

"Like a king," he said.

I glanced down at the costume. After telling him about the banquet when I got home from school yesterday, he drove me to the costume shop. I found a King Arthur costume with a jeweled crown and plastic sword.

"Maybe it's time I got more involved with your school activities," Dad said, smiling as I marched around the room.

"Well, Mom is the one who usually helps at school," I explained. "Of course, I'm really too old now for that kind of stuff anyway."

He shook his head. "You're never too old for your parents to be involved in your life. I should join the PTA. Carlos's father mentioned there was a meeting last week. He said I would have found it very interesting."

I glanced out the window, then grinned at him. "It was just another boring meeting."

"It's almost seven o'clock. I'll drive you to the school."

We walked past the ficus tree and outside to the car. Dad was reciting "Old King Cole" and laughing. I adjusted my crown as I slid into the front seat.

"Dad, what if the people you're leading don't want to be led?"

"For me, a great leader is someone who works to make things better, who's fair, and who isn't in it for the power," he said. "People want to be led into a better life, not led by the nose."

"You mean being too bossy?"

He glanced sideways at me and winked. "Yeah, something like that. Hey, do we need to pick up Lester and Carlos on the way?"

I shook my head. "They said they'd meet me there. They were a little upset that I didn't invite them as guests, but—"

"You didn't invite your best buddies?"

"Da-a-ad, they understand. They'll be great entertainers. I can always expect lots of fun when they're around."

"Oh. Well, I hope you know what you're doing," Dad said.

When we arrived at the school, I opened the door and hopped out. I leaned inside the car window. "Thanks. For the costume. And, for just being my dad."

"It's a dirty job, but someone's got to do it," Dad said with a grin.

I grinned back and moved away from the car. "Don't forget to water Mom's ficus!" I yelled.

After adjusting my crown and sword, I patted my royal robe and strode into the school. When I peeked through the cafeteria windows, I saw that there were candles everywhere. I was surprised that Dragon Lady Winthrop would allow them, but Mr. Bailey probably had lots of adults to chaperone.

"Invitation?" Mrs. Strauss, the librarian, asked as I opened the door to the cafeteria.

"*I'm* the king," I said. "I don't need an invitation."

"Oops, didn't recognize you. There are so many costumed kids running around in there," she said, squinting into my face. "Welcome, Your Majesty."

I waved a hand at her and strode grandly into the cafeteria.

The cafeteria looked terrific. The tables had been arranged into a big U shape. Two chairs draped in red velvet waited at the head of the tables. Several of the invited kids had already arrived and were sitting in their seats, drinking punch from plastic goblets. Most of the kids wore homemade costumes. Some wore silly hats with feathers; others wore tights under dresses or shorts.

Two tables were piled with turkey legs, bread, fruit . . . things everyone could eat with their hands.

I recognized some parents from the PTA, standing beside the tables as if ready to serve. Purple crepe paper hung from each corner of the ceiling and met in the middle. I remembered reading that dogs roamed the room during banquets at the castles, fighting over scraps. I wasn't surprised that the PTA had left that part out.

Lester and Carlos were nowhere in sight. I hoped they wouldn't be late.

Mr. Bailey stood in the corner of the cafeteria, talking with the PTA president. I wondered how he'd talked Mrs. Dollahan into having the PTA chaperone the dinner, especially after my interruption at the last meeting.

"Cool costume," Ernie Foster said. "Thanks a lot for inviting me. I'm Lord Ernie tonight."

I gave him a kingly wave. "No problem. You could return the favor by introducing me to your father sometime."

Ernie pushed back the cape that hung over his arm. "My dad?"

"Yeah," I said. "He manages the sporting goods store at the mall. I'd like to find out what kind of discount he'd give the school on some quality gym equipment."

"Well, you could talk to him at the store. He's there in the evenings and on Saturdays," Ernie said.

I shook my head. "It would be better if you would introduce me. You know, back me up about how awful our gym equipment is and how important it is that we get new stuff."

Willie stepped in between us. He huffed and puffed into my face. "Your Majesty, dinner is about to start and your jesters aren't here to entertain your royal guests."

"They'll be here, don't get your tights in a bunch," I said.

Ernie giggled and walked away.

I frowned at my knight. "Thanks a lot. I was finally making some headway on the gym equipment issue until you interrupted. I wonder who I could talk to about the ice-cream machine? If I changed it to lowfat yogurt, maybe Mrs. Winthrop would go for it."

Willie bowed and mumbled, "Sorry to interrupt. I just thought that you needed to know."

Willie walked away. He had created a quieter costume than the garbage-can suit he'd worn to the PTA meeting. He wore a shiny silver shirt and pants, something he must have put together himself, judging by the uneven staples surrounding the hems.

I looked around the room. These kids were the kind of friends a king and future student council president should have. They had parents who had positions, money, and power that I could use. None of them were as fun as Carlos and Lester, but funny friends never got a candidate votes. Unless they were famous *and* funny.

"Behold the queen," a voice shouted.

Music filled the cafeteria. Priscilla came into the cafeteria with a large boom box. Andrea stepped from a side door, followed by a growing crowd of giggling girls. She swished her skirt as she passed by me, waving like the queen of England to everyone in the room.

Two of her ladies-in-waiting walked around the room holding up a poster that said: TODAY'S QUEEN, TOMORROW'S PRESIDENT.

"Good grief," I groaned, forcing a smile. I couldn't let the voters think I was worried about Andrea. Even though I was.

Mr. Bailey rang a cowbell. "Hear ye! Hear ye! In honor of King Justin and Queen Andrea, you all are invited to the tables. Begin the feast."

"Great, time to eat," I said, walking to the head of the table. I winked at Andrea as we sat on our "thrones." She flashed a smile at me. It was all a part of her show since everyone was watching us.

She leaned over and said, "I am going to win

this student council election by a landslide, you know."

I waved my hand at the roomful of students. "Not if I can help it. Just wait and see. I can talk anyone into anything. I'll keep my promises and everyone will be fighting over who votes for me first."

"In your dreams," Andrea said. "How could they refuse such a great queen? I know what Marie Antoinette's problem was. She wanted them all to have cake when they were too poor to buy real food. But I'll get them things they really need, like perfumed soap in the bathroom and music over the loudspeakers and—"

"Where's Priscilla?" I interrupted.

Andrea wrinkled her nose. "I don't know. I may have to find another knight. She's not the greatest campaign manager. She's running for class secretary and will be too busy with her own campaign to help mine."

I glanced at Willie. He moved from one table to the next, straightening the plates and silverware. He helped pour punch into people's mugs. I had a feeling he was doing a little campaigning while he worked.

"Cool," Andrea said, pointing toward the back doors.

Parents, dressed in long black robes tied at the waist, filed out of the kitchen and placed more trays of food on the tables. I'd never seen so much good food in the school cafeteria. Come to think of it, I'd never seen *any* good food in the cafeteria before.

Willie sat in the chair beside me. "They look more like executioners than medieval waiters."

I laughed. "That was actually funny," I said aloud.

"Speaking of funny," Andrea said. "Where are those two goof-off friends of yours? I promised my guests entertainment."

I gnawed on a juicy turkey leg. I didn't want to admit to Andrea that I wasn't sure they were really coming. Maybe they were too angry about not being invited as guests. I started to tell her not to worry, when the doors of the cafeteria burst open.

"There they are!" I said. "I knew they'd be here."

Carlos and Lester marched into the room. They both smiled at me. I grinned and waved them over. But my smile faded when I saw the crowd pouring in behind them. Especially when I saw Badger standing beside Carlos. My jesters had betrayed me.

Chapter 19

♛

How Revolting Peasants Can Be

Future Politician's Rule #19—
Keep your voters happy!

I jumped up as the crowd spilled into the cafeteria. My crown tumbled to the floor and rolled under the table. Willie picked it up and placed it back on my head.

Andrea stood beside me, her hands on her hips. "Hey, this is only for invited guests. Mr. Bailey said so."

Carlos walked across the room, stopped in front of us, and folded his arms. "We, the peasants of Baileyland, are fed up. This is a mutiny."

"We're not on a boat, you know," Willie said. "The word is *revolution*."

Carlos frowned. "Okay, revolution, rebellion, or riot. Whatever you want to call it, we're doing it. We need a new coach . . . er . . . I mean king."

My eyes widened.

"The king orders you to leave right now!" I demanded. I looked into Carlos's eyes. "Please?"

Carlos just shook his head. "Sorry, you may be my buddy, but you're a lousy king. It's unanimous."

I couldn't believe that Carlos and Lester would go this far against me. It was embarrassing. And more than that, it hurt.

The mob filled the room and grabbed food from the tables. They laughed and shouted while the chaperones ran around trying to restore order.

I recognized most of the party crashers. They were the ones Andrea and I had thrown into the dungeon and the kids from Mr. Bailey's class who weren't invited to the feast. I was never so happy to have teachers and parents nearby.

Andrea grabbed me by the collar of my kingly costume. "Your friends are ruining our party!"

I jerked away. "Please, don't touch my royalness. And it's not all my fault. You made lots of people mad. All you cared about was being popular and bossy."

"Look who's talking," she shouted. "You and

your dumb speeches and your promises for music during tests and ice-cream machines and that silly fight to get the boys their own expensive gym equipment. No one cares about that stuff, they just care about how much fun they're having."

Andrea stood up and waved her arms. "If you want parties, vote for Queen Andrea as your student council president. I was just kidding about the dungeon and carrying my books and serving my lunch. I'm lots of fun. Really I am." She smiled at the crowd.

Christopher Poole moved in front of the others. "Off with her head!" He shouted.

Badger pointed to me. "Off with *his* head!"

Andrea sat back down. Mr. Bailey walked over to Christopher and Badger and whispered something. They both nodded and went back to eating.

I looked around the room. Everyone was laughing and grabbing at the free food. I fell into my throne and sighed. Had I wanted change or just power?

A chant began somewhere in the crowd.

"No more king. No more queen. Freedom is ours!"

It was quickly picked up by others, and before long, the room echoed with the voices. I saw that Mrs. Winthrop had even joined them. Badger sat in a chair holding a plate piled with meat and cheese. He pointed a turkey leg at me as he joined the chant.

"NO MORE KING. NO MORE QUEEN. FREEDOM IS *OURS!*"

Everyone cheered and whistled, even the kids sitting at the tables who were invited.

"Listen to me, people!" I shouted.

If anyone heard, they ignored me. Parents and teachers rushed in with extra chairs.

An awful truth hit me. There had been lots more food here than was needed for twenty guests, a king, and a queen. Maybe the adults had known this would happen.

A crowd gathered around Mr. Bailey. Lester and Carlos were right in the middle. Mr. Bailey nodded, then walked over to me and Andrea.

He bowed and grinned at us. "I'm sorry to do this, your royal majesties, but your people have ordered that, as part of their revolution—"

I leaned forward, nearly falling out of my throne. "Ordered what?"

"That the two of you are to lay down your crowns and sit with the commoners," Mr. Bailey said. "There will be no king and queen tonight."

Andrea yanked off her crown and threw it on the table. "What do I care? It's still a party. And I'm still running for fifth-grade president."

She stood up and stomped to the other side of the room to sit with her ladies-in-waiting. I could hear her sniffling as she walked away.

As the rest of my classmates found seats at the tables, I glanced at Mr. Bailey and waited for him to come to my rescue and change his mind. But he just smiled and held out his hand. I gave him my crown. This wasn't part of my plan at all.

How could Mr. Bailey have let this happen to us? He planned this project and expected us to do it for two weeks, didn't he?

"But, we're not finished with the project," I protested. "You're letting them kick us out?"

Mr. Bailey nodded, as if *he* had a plan, too.

Chapter 20

♛

De-Throne IS Gone

Future Politician's Rule #20—
Don't cry in front of the troops.

Everyone in Mr. Bailey's classroom stopped talking when I walked in Wednesday morning after gym.

I could see that something was different. Something was missing. I wasn't sure what it was until I walked over to my desk. At least, where my desk had been for the past week and a half.

My desk was gone. So was Andrea's.

I looked around the room. It looked almost like it did before the project started. There were more desks in the main part of the room than there were the day before—desks and kids who should have still been inside the dungeon.

The dungeon was its original size, the way it had been before Andrea and I threw so many kids inside that it had grown three times. I looked inside. Yes, there was my desk—beside Andrea's.

And a third. Willie waved at me.

Andrea sat in her chair, brushing her hair, stopping occasionally to scowl at our classmates.

"I'm afraid you've been overthrown, Justin," Mr. Bailey said. "For the remainder of the day, you and Andrea will sit in the dungeon. I'm declaring the project officially over at the end of class today."

"They weren't the king and queen you thought they'd be, were they?" Christopher asked.

Mr. Bailey smiled. "Actually, they were *exactly* the king and queen I thought they'd be. I expected them to get overthrown."

Badger shook his head. "Huh?"

"Power is a difficult thing if not handled correctly," Mr. Bailey explained. "There have been both good and bad rulers in history."

I folded my arms. "And I've been a lousy one."

"We," Andrea corrected me. She always had to compete, even in being insulted.

Mr. Bailey came to my side and put a hand on my shoulder. "Think about it awhile. Why were you and Andrea bad rulers in the end? Were your intentions good? Everyone who has played a part in this project has ideas on what was done right or wrong, or what could have been done differently. Think about your motives and your leaders' motives. You have the rest of the day and tomorrow to write your reports. Be honest. Don't just blame your king and queen. You went along with everything. Did you try to influence them to be better leaders or encourage their corruption? You have the rest of the hour to get started."

I glanced at my classmates. Had I really become a corrupt monarch? I was only trying to help.

I walked to my desk and plopped into the chair. Everyone knew I'd failed. All I could do was hide in my own dungeon.

I turned to Willie and frowned. "Why are *you* in here? Did Priscilla buy her way out?"

Willie shook his head. "Only you and Andrea were put into the dungeon. But a knight should always stand by his king, for better or worse."

I sighed. My best buddies hadn't stuck by me, but Willie, the person I'd taken advantage of and wished I hadn't chosen as my knight had been there for me to the end.

I pulled out a piece of paper and began writing questions:

A. Why couldn't I find a way to keep all the promises I made to everyone? Would I be able to keep promises as student council president?

B. Why didn't my friends understand that using this to help my campaign was my first priority? I was doing it all for them, too.

C. What is being a leader really all about?

D. Do I even have a chance now to win the election, or will Andrea be the fifth-grade president?

I had a lot to think about. After all, the president didn't run the country alone. He had committees and congressional people and secretaries and members of the Senate and on and on. Everyone threw in their ideas and opinions. Willie had tried to get me to listen.

I really wanted to be a good leader. I'd hurt my friends and they betrayed me. Andrea slipped in as a candidate and upstaged me more than once.

Maybe my classmates could be a part of my plan for a better and fairer school. Maybe the PTA hadn't taken me seriously because I didn't present my ideas in a way that would help and benefit *everyone*. After all, how seriously could you take a guy in a bathrobe when he brought along a three-ring circus? Maybe Andrea and I could work together to do something special for the school.

I turned to the next page in my notebook. A blank page.

I bent forward and wrote until my fingers hurt. By the time the bell rang for lunch, I had written five pages of my new plan.

Chapter 21

♛

One for All and All for One

Future Politician's Rule #21—
There *is* always enough
power to share.

I wasn't king anymore. The Triangles didn't invite me to sit with them at lunch. No one bowed or called me "Your Majesty" when we passed in the hall.

It had been fun being so popular. And so powerful. But everyone had used me as much as I'd used them. Mr. Bailey's project showed us all how easy it was for monarchies to become self-centered and corrupt. I didn't want to admit to a teacher that he'd taught me more than I'd ever learned from reading books on politics or listening to speeches.

So I didn't.

But one thing was for sure, I was yesterday's news. If I wanted to win this student council election, I had to show everyone that I was there to help, not rule.

Willie still hung around me, which wasn't a bad thing. In his pushy, weird way, he knew what I really wanted to do all along—to be a good leader.

I was still upset at Carlos and Lester, but after a couple of days, I thought that I might have done the same if I'd been bossed around by my best friend. After school, I shared a bag of Jelly Beans with Carlos, Lester, and Willie. I apologized to them all.

Carlos punched my arm like old times. "I guess we'd have gone power hungry, too. I sure was ready to trade you to another team, though."

Lester gave Willie a punch.

Willie glanced at me. I nodded. He punched Lester back.

It was good to be just Justin again.

Future student council president.

I had let all that kingly power go to my head. I made so many crazy promises I couldn't keep up with trying to make them come true.

"Hey, kid, let's go. Now."

I looked up at the sound of Badger's voice. The second grader I'd seen him with before was standing under a tree in front of the school. He picked his books off the ground and walked over to Badger. I couldn't keep wild promises, but maybe there were some things I could take leadership over.

"I'll be back," I told my friends, and ran across the school grounds. My heart was pounding, but I'd had enough of Badger bullying this little kid.

"Why don't you leave him alone and pick on someone your own size?" I gasped.

Badger stared at me. "Mind your own business."

I grabbed the little kid's arm. "Come on, we'll go see Mrs. Winthrop and stop Badger from picking on you. I'll walk you home if you want, or back to Donna Park Elementary."

The kid pulled away from me. "Leave me alone. Hey, weren't you that king guy? I heard you got kicked out."

I folded my arms. "Listen, I'm just trying to help you. What's Badger doing? Stealing your lunch money? Making you do his chores?"

The kid shook his head. "Badger's my friend. He . . ."

Badger made a move for the kid. "Wait, don't say . . ."

I stepped between them. "You can't tell him what to say. Go on, kid, spill your guts."

The boy smiled at Badger. "He's my hero. He's helping me with my reading."

I looked from the kid to Badger. "What?"

"I'm dyslexic," the kid said. "Badger is the best tutor I ever had."

Badger's face turned red. "Let's go," he said. He and the kid walked to their bus. I stared after them. I wondered what else Badger might be hiding.

On Saturday, I called Carlos, Lester, and Willie and asked them to meet me at the mall.

"What's up?" Carlos asked. "The mall doesn't open for thirty minutes."

"I know," Justin said. "But I want to talk about my new plan. I really want your help this time. And your opinions. I don't want Andrea to know about this yet. Just listen and tell me what you think."

Lester slapped his hands against his face and staggered around, collapsing on the steps to the mall's entrance. "Oh no, another plan. Call the air force. Call the marines. Call me a pizza."

"You're a pizza," Carlos mumbled.

Willie laughed and slapped Carlos on the back. Carlos frowned at Willie, then smiled. I had never heard Willie really laugh at a joke before. And I couldn't remember when Willie had last sniffled or whined. I was glad he was there.

"Be serious for a minute," I said. "I discovered a lot of things this week. A good leader doesn't accomplish things on his own."

"Yeah," Carlos said. "But what's all that got

to do with coming to the mall?"

I pulled a handful of folded papers from my back pocket. "I need you to split up and take these to the managers of every store in the mall. This little paper, and a lot of teamwork from the kids at school, is going to help us get our gym equipment *and* replace the school's trees."

I held out one of the papers for everyone to see.

PAYTON INTERMEDIATE SCHOOL
 NEEDS YOU!
We need trees.
We need bushes.
We need flowers.
AND
We NEED new gym equipment for the
 boys.
YOU need advertising.
Call Justin Davies at 555-4312 and find
 out how you can help the kids of
 your community
AND
get yearlong advertising.
Let's all work together for a better
 tomorrow for our kids.
Be the first to join People for Payton!

"A better tomorrow for our kids?" Carlos asked.

Willie yanked the paper from my hand. "It's very adult sounding. I'm sure the business leaders will take you seriously."

"Thanks," I said. I split the flyers four ways. "Come with me while I do the first one."

"Gee, Justin, don't you think we can pass out a piece of paper by ourselves?" Carlos asked. He shook the flyers in my face.

I backed away. I was doing it again, trying to take charge. "Sure, you can. But I thought that if you heard me give my speech, it would make more sense. But you can give your own speech any way you want."

Carlos grinned.

Lester nodded. "Sure, we can be heroes together. We'll be like the great old comedy teams. Hope and Crosby. Martin and Lewis. Rocky and Bullwinkle."

Willie gave me a thumbs-up. "We're beside you, King Justin."

I shuddered. "Don't ever call me that again."

Willie nodded. "I promise." Then he reached into his pocket and pulled out something that he pushed into each of our hands. "I had these made yesterday. I've made seventy-five of them to pass out at school."

I stared at the button in my hand and turned it over. My face stared back at me. A grotesque, grimacing face. Above it, in bold black letters, were the words: VOTE FOR JUSTIN DAVIES, STUDENT

COUNCIL PRESIDENT! "Where did you get this picture?" I gasped. My face on the buttons looked as if I'd eaten snails for breakfast.

Willie grinned. "I took it at the joust. It's not your best look, is it?" He put a piece of paper in my hand. "Oh yes, here's the bill. It's $54.85. I can take a check."

Carlos and Lester laughed and pinned the buttons to their shirts. "At least no one will forget you, Justin."

"Just great, an unforgettable mug shot," I said, leading the way into the mall.

The first business we came to was a shoe store. I marched around the shoe displays to the cash register. A man with his hair in a ponytail and a gold hoop in one earlobe was sorting a box of leggings. "I'd like to speak to the manager."

The man raised an eyebrow and leaned over to stare into my eyes. "What for?"

"I'd just like to talk to the manager about a business proposition," I explained.

"Oh, well, let's hear it."

I looked around the store. "Uh, I'd rather talk to the manager."

The man grinned. He reached up and tweaked the earring. "You're talking to him, kid."

"Oh," I said. I placed one of the flyers on the desk beside the cash register and waited while the man looked it over.

"So, what's the scam?"

"Oh, no scam, sir," Willie said quickly. "My buddy, Justin, is honest and trustworthy. He'll be a much respected political official someday."

I turned to the store manager. "Listen, here's the deal. Our school was vandalized a few weeks ago. Someone mangled and destroyed all our plants. Trees, flowers, shrubs . . . everything. The PTA has been trying to find a way to raise money to replace them."

I pointed to my friends. "My buddies and I are part of the fifth-grade class that would like to help. We're going to put on a special fair in one week, on Saturday, to raise money for the new trees and flowers. How would you like to see your business's name on a plaque near a beautiful maple? Kids would see it all the time. Kids buy lots of shoes."

The manager tugged at the earring. "So, what do you want from me? If *you're* raising the money, where do I come in? I'm sure you're not just going to give me this advertising for nothing."

I smiled. "You're very wise, sir. The boys' PE equipment at Payton is a joke. Old, out of date . . . it really needs to be replaced."

With a laugh, the manager held the paper out to me. "Sorry, kid, I know I can't get the owner to agree to buy your school new gym equipment."

I shook my head. "Of course not. But, you

could get him to donate, say, a pair of shoes? At the end of the fair, we'll have an auction to raise the money for the equipment."

The manager stared at me. Then, he smiled. "You know, you're a pretty resourceful kid. Okay, leave me the flyer and I'll see what I can do."

I winked at Carlos, then shook the manager's hand.

Willie patted my shoulder. "I'm honored to be a part of this. What a remarkable idea."

"Yeah, way cool," Lester agreed. "But, how are you going to get the other kids to agree to be a part of this fair? Especially the girls."

I smiled. "I've got a plan."

Chapter 22

♔

A Festival of Heroes

Future Politician's Rule #22—
Speak loudly and carry
a large plan.

unday afternoon I dialed the phone three times and hung up every time Andrea answered before I finally said, "Hello, Andrea?"

"Justin? Are you the goon who keeps calling me and hanging up?" Andrea shouted into the phone.

"Sorry," I said. "I guess my hand slipped." Or maybe my nerve slipped. "Listen, Andrea, I think you and I need to form a truce until the elections. I have an idea of something we can all do to help the school."

Andrea laughed. "Uh-oh, you have an idea? What is it?"

"Just meet me in the courtyard at lunch on Monday. Bring your friends." I hung up before she could turn it into a long argument.

I rode my bicycle to Willie's house. Willie had offered to let me use his computer to print out invitations to our classmates. It explained about the special meeting during Monday's lunch. I was actually looking forward to going to his house this time. He had some great books on politics I was hoping to borrow.

"Hi," Willie said when he opened the front door. "My mom's taking a nap, so we'll need to be quiet going to my room."

"Got anything to snack on?" I asked.

Willie put his fingers to his lips and whispered, "Oh no, I'm not allowed to have food in my room. Although, I must admit, I do have a stash of granola bars in my dresser."

"The kind with fruit or chocolate in them?"

"No, just plain granola. They're better for you."

I followed Willie to his room. We worked on the invitations until I held a stack of neatly printed cards:

IT'S TIME TO ACT!
WHAT IS PAYTON INTERMEDIATE
    SCHOOL?

IT'S ME! IT'S YOU! IT'S US!
WE ARE A DEMOCRACY, A FREE
*   SCHOOL IN A FREE LAND.*
WE ARE NOT RULED, WE ARE LED!
WE ARE NOT PEASANTS WITHOUT
*   POWER!*
THIS IS THE TIME TO RALLY TOGETHER
*   AND COME TO THE AID OF YOUR*
*   SCHOOL!*
BE A HERO AND HAVE A BLAST DOING IT!
COME TO A MEETING IN THE COURT-
*   YARD DURING C LUNCH.*
BRING YOUR IMAGINATION!

I stuck the invitations in my back pocket, thanked Willie, and biked all the way home. My plans for being a hero had definitely changed. Or maybe I understood again what I really wanted to do. I didn't want to be a leader for the power, well, not completely. I wanted to bring changes that would help people. I wanted to follow after some of my heroes: George Washington, Abraham Lincoln, and the man who became a city council-man so he could help build safer playgrounds in our district.

I wanted to be the kind of leader people would remember because I made life a little better. My first step was to get the fifth graders at Payton behind my new idea.

Monday morning, I stood at the school's entrance and passed out invitations to everyone in Mr. Bailey's class, plus a dozen other kids who had really gotten interested in the project.

We had early lunch, and I reached the courtyard before the lunch bell stopped ringing. Willie, Carlos, and Lester ran in and high-fived their ex-king. Before long, the courtyard was crowded.

"What's going on, Davies?"

"Who died and left you boss?"

"Yeah, you're not king anymore."

I stood on a cement bench and held up my hands for quiet. "Listen, everyone. I know how we can replace the trees, get new gym equipment for the boys, and have a great Halloween party that lasts all day."

"The party part sounds cool, but isn't it the parents' and teachers' job to figure out how to make the school look good?" Christopher asked.

"What about the environment?" Priscilla said. "That's important. The trees and bushes aren't just to make the school pretty."

I blinked in surprise, and when Priscilla smiled at me, I smiled back.

Andrea stepped in front of Priscilla. "Why should the girls work to help the guys get stuff? I'm busy with my campaign." She turned to the crowd. "Remember, vote for me, the people's president, next Monday at the student council elections. A vote for Andrea is a vote for your-self."

She held out a tote bag and began pulling out small sacks of candy. She shoved one in my hand. It had a picture of her on the bag and neatly printed words: "Vote for Sweet Andrea." I groaned as kids started stuffing candy in their mouths.

I hesitated. There were only seven campaign days left. Shouldn't I spend them making sure I had votes?

I grabbed one of the sacks and said, "A truce, Andrea. Just listen to my idea and see what you think. I bet you can come up with some good ones, too."

Andrea stared at me a minute, then nodded. She stuffed the sacks back into her tote bag. "So, what's the idea?"

Willie nudged me. "Go on. Convince them that this is important. You can do it."

Willie was right. I didn't just want to be a politician. I wanted to be a good one. I waved my arms for attention, then put my fingers in my mouth and whistled. "Haven't you ever wanted to do something just because it was a good thing? This school gives us a lot. We should give something back."

Badger pushed his way through the crowd. Like the Red Sea, the other kids parted. "What's the school giving to us?"

"An education," Willie said.

I pointed to Lester. "You want to be an astronaut someday, right?"

"Hey, he's already deep in space," Carlos said, giving Lester a friendly shove.

"My head's full of space," Lester added.

"You can't be an astronaut without knowing math and science," I explained. Then, I whirled and pointed dramatically at Badger. "What do *you* want to do?"

Everyone turned toward Badger. The courtyard was so quiet I could hear my heart throbbing. I knew there was more to Badger than a growl and big fists.

Badger shrugged. "I want to write books . . . scary adventures and about guys meeting aliens and going to exciting places." He clutched his red notebook and looked down.

I couldn't believe it. Badger wanted to be an author like Bruce Coville or Ray Bradbury or Stephen King. So his notebook wasn't a hit list after all. I bet no one else but me knew that he was tutoring a second grader.

"Then you definitely need English classes," I said.

Badger scratched his head. "Yeah, so what does that have to do with gym equipment?"

"Healthy bodies bring strong minds," Willie shouted.

Badger stared at me. I stared back. A slow

grin started on his face. "I never thought about it that way. I just thought of school as keeping me from having more time to write my stories."

"Just think, you'd be known as one of the kids who made a big difference at Payton. Have a goal and a plan."

Badger pounded his fist against his notebook. "A plan to write? Cool idea."

My heart beat faster. Badger had actually listened to me. I turned back to the crowd. "We'd be the fifth-grade class everyone remembered!" I shouted. No one spoke. I had their attention.

"This is the plan," I said, lowering my voice for dramatic effect. "We're going to have the coolest fall festival ever. It will be a medieval fair and an auction to raise money for new trees and gym equipment. Everyone will play an important part. No one will hog the show."

Andrea moved to stand beside me. "And who will be the king and queen of the festival . . . hmm?"

I glanced at the other kids. "Just for the sake of the party, I thought we'd get back into our roles. But just for the fun of the day."

Andrea nodded. "I don't care about the boys' gym equipment, but it would be nice to have the school look pretty again. And it does sound like fun." She grinned at me. "What great publicity for my campaign."

I shook my head. "This isn't about anyone's campaign. Truce, remember?"

Andrea folded her arms. "Okay, sure. Just until the end of the festival."

"Deal," I said.

The crowd moved closer. I asked Badger if he would take notes about the ideas everyone had for the parts they would play. Badger opened his red notebook and began to write.

Chapter 23

♛

Hear Ye! Hear Ye!

Future Politician's Rule #23—The operative word is . . . publicity!

When George Washington led his troops into battle, it couldn't have been as exciting as the time after school and on weekends that I spent with my friends, classmates, and even Badger, working on the fair. Willie, Lester, and Carlos came over almost every day to help plan. We even invited Andrea and Priscilla. Andrea and I agreed to have a truce on campaigning until after the fair.

Badger held up the signs he'd been creating.

BE *FAIR* TO YOUR SCHOOL! COME TO THE MEDIEVAL *FAIRE* & AUCTION!

SUPPORT PAYTON! SEE AMAZING JUGGLERS, DRAMATIC ACTORS, AND WATCH A SPINE-TINGLING JOUST AT THE MEDIEVAL FAIRE THIS SATURDAY!

"Wow, Badger, you really *should* be a writer," I said. "These are great."

Badger grinned, and this time it wasn't scary.

We put signs up all over town. Sheila Branson even got her uncle, who owns a radio station, to let me go on the air and give my pitch for the fair and auction.

Andrea and I met at the radio station Thursday after school. It was only two days until the fair. And just four days until the school election.

"Andrea, we have to do this right. No arguing."

Andrea nodded. "You can do a lot of the talking, just give me some time, too."

I agreed. I had a six-page speech prepared. I hadn't told Andrea about that part.

The DJ, on the other hand, was more interested in the importance of being loud, excited, and brief. The first two were easy. Brief wasn't exactly a part of my vocabulary.

"Okay, kid, just tell us the whys and whens," Crazy Calvin said, shoving a mike in my face.

I grabbed the microphone and cleared my throat. "Well, Cal, we, the fifth-grade class of Payton Intermediate School, are here, represented by me, Justin Davies, future city councilman and president—"

Andrea leaned in front of the mike. "And Andrea Carey, the down-to-earth friend of the students—"

Crazy Calvin snatched the microphone back. "Um, yes, please get to the point." He covered the microphone and whispered, "The name's Crazy Calvin. Not Cal. Don't forget."

I nodded. Politicians had to keep the media happy.

"Anyway, Crazy Calvin, our school needs new shrubs and trees. We need a green environment. To do our part for the environment, we are having the coolest carnival in the whole state of Texas. All the money will go to buying the school new greenery. And our class will do the planting, too. We're willing to put aside our homework to toil in the soil."

I paused for dramatic effect. Crazy Calvin opened his eyes as if he'd been sleeping. Then they went wide. "Hey, kid, you got dead air!"

I leaned closer to the microphone. "Oops, sorry Cal . . . I mean, Crazy Cal . . . Crazy Calvin. Okay, so everyone come. Bring lots of money, because at the end of the fair, we're having an auction that you don't want to miss. We've got autographed shoes by sports greats, concert tickets, a pillow slept on by the mayor himself, and lots more."

Andrea cleared her throat. I had promised her some time, too. "And remember, the concession stands are sponsored by the 'Andrea Carey for Student Council President' campaign."

"Hey," I said, glaring at her. "No personal campaigning." This wasn't a good time for Andrea and me to debate. "So listen, everyone. Don't be a party pooper. Come find out what it's like to go back in time and see knights, fortune-tellers, magicians, jugglers, and the coolest king you'll ever meet. It's time to come to the aid of your school, your community, your kids, my political career—"

"Swell kid, we'll be there. Thanks for stopping by—"

I grabbed the mike one more time. "Don't forget. This Saturday, October 31, at Payton Intermediate School. Bring money."

"Tons of it," Andrea added loudly.

Crazy Calvin wrestled the microphone out of my hand and shooed us out of the sound booth.

"Way to hog the mike," Andrea said as we walked outside.

I shrugged. "Sorry, speeches are in my blood. I can't help it."

Andrea pulled a folded sheet of paper from her pocket. "Great, then you can read mine. I stuffed these in the fifth-grade lockers today." She turned and walked away.

I opened the paper and read:

HOW SHOULD YOU VOTE IN THE FIFTH-GRADE ELECTION? ANDREA CAREY LISTENS TO YOUR IDEAS. ANDREA CAREY WILL RULE THE FIFTH GRADE WITH FAIRNESS (I PROMISE THIS TIME). ANDREA IS THE SMART CANDIDATE, THE ONE WITH ALL A'S ON HER REPORT CARD. VOTE FOR THE CANDIDATE WITH A SWIMMING POOL IN HER BACKYARD.

Paid for by the Andrea Carey Campaign.

I stared at the paper. It had "Vote for Andrea" printed in the corners in red lettering. And everyone thought I was bossy.

"Thanks a lot, Andrea," I said to the empty street.

I tried to think about the carnival on the way home, but all I could hear was Andrea's victory speech.

Chapter 24

♔

Dunk the King and Save a Tree!

Future Politician's Rule #24— Do whatever it takes to win and have fun doing it.

R ed and yellow leaves decorated the streets when Dad and I drove to the school on Saturday. Thanks to my classmates and the town businessmen, in a few years Payton Intermediate School would once again have tall trees to give shade in the spring, bright leaves in the fall, and a place to hide behind while throwing winter snowballs. Even Priscilla's father came through and donated the wood and paint for the booths. He also agreed to match whatever we raised at the auction for the gym equipment.

Dad was a great help. He and some of the other fathers built all the booths. And Dad donated two of his hand-carved ships to the auction.

By the time we drove into the school parking lot, the fair was already busy with activity.

Mrs. Winthrop agreed to hold the festival in the field behind the school. She had patted me on the shoulder and blubbered like a baby when Andrea and I told her about the idea . . . my idea. It was hard to call her the Dragon Lady after that.

"This is so great, Dad," I said, jumping out of the car.

At a large cardboard replica of castle doors, Mr. Bailey lowered the drawbridge and welcomed us inside.

"I'm the castle guard," he explained, showing off his gray leotard, black shorts, a gray pullover, and a bright red hood that fit tight against his head. "I've always wanted an excuse to wear this," he said, patting the silver-mail shirt. He pointed to the little chain links. "I watched a guy make this. I bought it at a Renaissance festival years ago. Don't know why, just thought it was a great thing to have."

Dad and Mr. Bailey shook hands. "I guess just about everyone in town is talking about this," Dad said.

Mr. Bailey put his hand on my shoulder. "It's the most exciting thing I've seen at this school in a long time. Justin worked hard—you must be proud."

"I am," Dad said, winking at me. "I think we're looking at the next student council president. Then, city councilman . . . and, after that . . . who knows."

"President and world ruler," I suggested.

Mr. Bailey bowed. Instead of blowing a horn, he played a kazoo to announce each guest.

Dad went to talk to Mrs. Winthrop while I went into the school to change into my king's costume. When everyone begged Andrea and me to play our parts one more time, I felt honored. Then I discovered the plan was for me and my queen to be the guests of honor at the dunking booth.

By the time I put on my costume and returned to the festival, crowds of kids, parents, and teachers were spending money on games and shows.

Andrea waited for me at the dunking booth. She shook her head at the crowd.

"Believe me, I'll remember everyone who dunks me," she warned.

I couldn't wait to see her take a dive in the dunking pool.

"The dunking booth will open in thirty minutes. You can buy your tickets at the ticket booth. Remember, it's for the school," I told the waiting crowd. "Don't be stingy."

I grabbed Andrea's arm. "We should walk around and encourage people to spend more money."

We walked through the festival, stopping at the different shows so that I could give a pep talk. Okay, one of my speeches.

"Ooh, doesn't he look disgusting," Andrea said. She pointed toward a tree where a grimy kid dressed in rags leaned against the trunk.

I moved closer. "Willie?"

The mud-streaked face peeked up at me from a torn hat. He grinned, held out his hat, and shouted, "Alms, my liege, alms for a poor beggar."

A glass jar behind Willie had already begun to fill with coins. I gave him a thumbs-up. He was the best beggar ever, and the best knight, too.

Shouts of laughter and applause drew me toward a crowd. I made my way through to the center, where Carlos and Lester were performing. Carlos, wearing a purple satin robe and pointed hat, declared himself court wizard. Lester danced around in his jester costume, interfering with Carlos's feats of magic, which never turned out as planned.

I walked past a tent where Priscilla sat waiting to tell fortunes. She smiled at me, then looked down into her glass ball. I tried to remember why I'd thought she was so snooty.

"How goes the future-telling business?" I asked Priscilla.

Priscilla waved her hands over the glass ball. She had rings on each of her fingers and plastic bracelets that clanked together as her arms moved.

"I see a crowded fair, a school with healthy new plants, and a boys' gym that matches the girls'." She glanced at Andrea. "And I see a wet queen."

Andrea snorted. "Yeah? And do you see a queen shoving her best friend in the moat?"

Priscilla shook her head. "No, that's not in the future. But I do see a kindly queen forgiving all who have offended her."

"And one who watches me give the acceptance speech for student council president," I said.

Andrea jabbed me with her elbow. "We'll see who's giving what speech."

We left the tent and I surveyed the kingdom. My kingdom.

"Hey, someone's fighting," Andrea said.

I turned and looked where Andrea pointed. The crowds blocked my view.

"I'll do it!" a voice yelled.

"No, me!"

I followed the sound of shouting until I came to the platform that had been built to be used as a stage. Danny and Brandon were arguing with each other while Marilee tried to pull them apart.

"What's the problem?" I yelled. "People are waiting for your play to start," I said. I still couldn't believe that Badger had written the play. It was good.

Danny poked a finger into Brandon's chest. "He thinks he's going to be the brave knight that rescues Princess Marilee from the dragon. I'm not playing a dragon."

"Well, neither am I!" Brandon shouted.

"Look, you're going to do two performances of the play . . . right?" I asked.

Danny and Brandon nodded.

"Then take turns," I said out loud. I walked away as Danny and Brandon began arguing over who would play the knight first.

I waved to Badger across the field. Badger had painted a large sign and hammered it to a pole: WORLD'S STRONGEST MAN!

He lifted weights and drew a crowd of girls by flexing his muscled arms.

I was glad that we were becoming friends. Especially since we were going to re-create our joust as the final event of the festival.

I walked back to the dunking booth. A crowd had gathered. They held out tickets and picked up beanbags to throw at the target, a metal arm attached to the seat. The water looked cold.

Andrea was the first to get dunked. Her crown floated in the water as she sputtered words that made some parents gasp and kids applaud.

Andrea climbed back into her chair and scowled at the crowd.

SPLASH!

Down she went again! I howled. How many enemies *did* Andrea have anyway?

"We're next," a familiar voice said.

Carlos and Lester stepped to the front of the line. They unfurled a roll of tickets long enough to touch the ground. "Isn't it about time for your royal bath, King Justin?" Carlos said.

I moved into the dunk tank and sat down as Lester flexed his arm. I closed my eyes as the ball hit the target. The water was *very* cold.

Chapter 25

♛

Politics Is My Game

Future Politician's Rule #25—
Always thank the little people.

What is your bid for a baseball and glove from Snyder's Toys?" Mrs. Winthrop shouted. "Remember, they've been signed by Nolan Ryan."

"I'll give you five bucks!"

"Seven!"

"Ten fifty!"

"I'll bid twenty dollars!"

"I've got twenty, do I hear twenty-five?" Mrs. Winthrop asked. "Who will help us buy new mats for the boys' gym?"

I shivered as a cool wind blew through the tent. My hair was still a little damp from my thirty-six dunkings, but at least I had on dry clothes. And now, the last of the auction items was about to be sold and I could go home and have a private celebration party alone with Dad. I couldn't wait to call Mom and tell her all about the fair.

Mrs. Winthrop told me that there had never been so much participation or attendance for any past school event. The final joust with Badger had drawn a bigger crowd than when the drama club and choir performed *The Sound of Music* last spring. Everyone rooted for both Badger and me until we each won a game.

Andrea closed the fun part of the festival with a dramatic reading about King Arthur. She was great. Even better than Marilee Cash.

Lester, Carlos, and Willie promised they'd help me with my campaign to become student council president, no matter what it took. Willie became a part of the group—a foursome had been created. My first promise to myself as president would be to listen to what the other kids had to say. It was the best way.

When the last item had been auctioned—a sweater that a former Miss Teen America had once owned—Mrs. Winthrop waved her arms and called for silence.

"There are two industrious students who put this event together with a great deal of creativity and teamwork. Justin Davies and Andrea Carey, will you please come on stage?"

I leaped onto the stage and pulled Andrea up with me. Mrs. Winthrop shook our hands as a reporter took our picture. I'd never shaken hands with a dragon. I grinned at her before turning to the crowd.

"We, the students at Payton Intermediate School, thank you all for coming to our festival. Mrs. Winthrop has let me know that we have raised enough money to replace all the trees, bushes, and flowers that were vandalized."

The tent filled with applause and cheering. I raised my hands in a victory salute. I imagined red, white, and blue streamers and balloons falling around me. I imagined hats, posters, and banners with my picture and name. I imagined the crowd going wild as the announcement was made that I, Justin Davies, was the new president of the United States.

I glanced at Andrea. She shook her head. "Go on, finish your speech."

"I also want to thank the businesses who donated to our auction," I shouted. "I feel sure, with the money Mr. Ashworth-Cole has agreed to include along with the discount Mr. Foster of Foster's Sporting Goods promised, that the guys of Payton will soon enjoy new, up-to-date, totally cool gym equipment. We might even let the girls visit."

Andrea groaned.

Another round of applause sounded through the tent, accented by whistles from the boys in the crowd.

"Last of all," I added, "I want to thank the fifth graders of Payton Intermediate School, who worked as a team to reach our goals. I'm proud to lead this once unruly, ragged bunch of . . ."

I stopped talking. The kids in the crowd moved in closer. "Uh, as I was saying, the greatest bunch of absolutely wonderful, talented, and helpful friends. And if you vote for me for fifth-grade student council president, this school will never be the same again."

Andrea snatched the microphone and said, "I'm also very proud to be your past queen and future class president. We are the best fifth graders Payton will ever have."

"Huzzah!" Willie shouted, and the crowd applauded.

Andrea curtsied. "When I'm fifth-grade president, I promise to take your ideas to Mrs. Winthrop, ideas to make life as a fifth grader at Payton the best ever."

I took the microphone back from Andrea. "My worthy opponent is right, you're all the best. And because of that, you need the best student council president. Remember, that's Justin on election day. J . . . U . . . S . . ."

Mrs. Winthrop wrestled the microphone

from my hand. "Thank you both, but we'll save those speeches for Election Day. Remember students, voting will be held on Monday."

Andrea leaned close to Mrs. Winthrop and shouted, "Don't forget to stop by the Andrea-for-President booth on Monday morning and pick up your free pen."

There was another cheer from the crowd. Andrea punched my arm. "You know, you really did a good thing, Justin. I hate to admit it, but you kept a big promise and we all had a great time being a part of it."

I slapped my hand against my forehead. "What? A compliment from Andrea? I must be dreaming."

She smiled. "I'm still going to win the election."

"In your dreams," I said, giving her a kingly bow. Then I bowed to Mrs. Winthrop and to the crowd. I took the crown from my head and threw it into the air. Someone caught it and threw it again. Like a beach ball, it flew from hand to hand.

"Justin. Justin. Justin!" I recognized Willie's voice starting the chant, and soon it grew stronger as others joined in.

Politics was as exciting as a roller-coaster ride. Maybe Mr. Bailey didn't plan this to happen; after all, he couldn't plan a project to change the life of every kid. But this one changed mine.

192

I glanced at Willie and grinned. He gave me a thumbs-up. I gave Carlos and Lester a high five, then jumped in the air with a loud whoop.

"The king is dead," I shouted. "Long live President Justin!"

In just two days, the voters would write down the names they wanted for class leaders. I glanced at Andrea. One of us had a big disappointment coming up on Monday. I hoped it wouldn't be me.

Chapter 26

♛

And the Winner IS . . .

Future Politician's Rule #26—
In victory or defeat, never give up hope!

Monday was the last day for campaigning. The school grounds were littered with flyers begging for votes. But none of the student council campaigns had been as wild as mine and Andrea's. It would go down in the history of Payton as the presidential race to end all presidential races.

Carlos and Lester threw confetti on the ground in front of me as I walked into the building.

Willie dragged in a helium gas tank. I wondered if I could give my acceptance speech in a helium voice.

I walked into the front office. Andrea was helping Mrs. Winthrop look through a nursery catalog and pick out new bushes and trees for the school. I caught Andrea's eye and smiled. She grinned back. I had to admit, she'd gotten more serious about helping the school since the fair.

She handed me a pen. It said: ANDREA CAREY RULES!

I gave it back and walked into the hall, nearly bumping into Willie holding a handful of ribbons attached to helium balloons. In bright black lettering the balloons said: VOTE FOR A WINNER!

"Thanks, Willie," I said.

Gym class went by like a blur. Coach kept patting my head and sniffling. "The new gym equipment arrives on Friday. I never believed you could really do it."

I waved to my classmates. "Remember who kept his promise when you vote today."

By the time the bell rang, I was starting to feel a little sick. Today was the day. In a few moments the ballots would be passed out. All the way to history class I smiled, shook hands, begged for votes, and made one more promise. I promised to be the best fifth-grade president they'd ever had. I didn't remind them they'd never had one before.

Carlos, Lester, Willie, and I walked into Mr. Bailey's class. Everything was back to normal.

No dungeon. No signs. I missed being king. But it was time to move on.

Badger gave me a thumbs-up. "You've got my vote."

I grinned. "Thanks."

Andrea laughed. "Well, that's one."

"One less for you," I added.

Willie walked over to Andrea and said, "That's two for Justin!"

"Sit," Mr. Bailey ordered.

Mrs. Winthrop began her morning announcements about today's lunch menu, the problem with kids running in the halls, and an announcement about the missing lizard in Mrs. Gray's science class.

"Your teachers will pass out voting ballots for fifth- and sixth-grade student councils," she continued. "At the beginning of fourth period, fifth graders will come to the auditorium where the results will be announced. Sixth-grade results will be announced during fifth period."

Mr. Bailey passed out the ballots as soon as Mrs. Winthrop stopped talking. "Fold and pass your ballots forward when you're done."

My hand shook as I stared at my name listed above Andrea's under *President—Fifth Grade*.

This was what I'd dreamed about since summer. I hoped I had learned enough to be a great leader. I think I had learned enough to be a good one. I was a born politician. But could I win my first election?

I checked the box beside my name.

When Mrs. Winthrop announced that "all fifth graders were to report to the auditorium," Lester, Carlos, and I shot out of fourth-period English before anyone else. Willie wasn't in our English class, but we saved a seat for him in the auditorium.

I stared at the four seats on stage. In a few moments, they would be filled with the new student council.

"Please, please let one of those chairs be mine," I whispered.

Lester elbowed me. "I hate to scare you, but I've talked to a lot of kids who said they were voting for Andrea. She had some good bribes. Doughnuts. Pens. A promise of a pool victory party in Priscilla's indoor pool."

Carlos licked his lips. "Yeah, those were some good doughnuts."

I glared at him.

Mrs. Winthrop tapped the microphone on the stage. "Sssh, students. We'll begin when you are quiet."

I jumped up and yelled, "Quiet!"

Willie slid into the seat next to Carlos as I sat down. He leaned over and whispered, "Save your voice for your victory speech, Justin."

I grinned. At least Willie hadn't been stuffing his face with Andrea's doughnuts. Then I saw the pen in his jacket pocket. He shrugged. "A free pen is a free pen."

A few of Willie's balloons floated around the auditorium. They were cooler than Andrea's pens anyway.

"I know you're anxious to meet your new student council, so I'll begin," Mrs. Winthrop said. "Fifth-grade student council treasurer is Nancy Gibbs."

A squeal came from the back corner. Nancy ran onto the stage and took the certificate Mrs. Winthrop held out.

"I'll guard any money we raise like it was my own," Nancy said with a giggle.

Willie nodded. "Her father is an accountant. I voted for her."

Nancy sat in one of the chairs as Mrs. Winthrop said, "Secretary for your fifth-grade student council is Austin Fowler."

Austin leaped onto the stage. He was the best baseball player in the whole school. He just shouted into the microphone, "Yay me!"

Willie nodded again. "He's got the best memory and will remember everything said at council meetings. Knows every baseball statistic. I voted for him."

Austin took his certificate and sat beside Nancy.

Mrs. Winthrop studied the paper in her hand. "Vice president was a bit of a surprise. We've never had a write-in winner before, but this student really pursued your votes. Your student council vice president is Willie Fisher."

I nearly fell out of my seat. Willie? When did he have time to campaign?

Willie shrugged. "Sorry I didn't tell you, Justin. I only decided to run at the carnival. Whenever anyone dropped a coin in my bucket, I gave them a card."

He handed me a business card as he ran onstage.

WILLIE FISHER, THE KING'S RIGHT-HAND MAN.

I grinned. The guy was amazing. A little bizarre but amazing. I wish he'd told me. I would've voted for him. I wondered if those balloons had been for my campaign or his?

There was one chair left on stage. I looked across the small auditorium. Andrea was practically bouncing in her seat.

Mrs. Winthrop leaned closer to the microphone. "And now, the final officer. This has been the most incredible campaign I have ever witnessed in a school. It was a very close race, I must tell you. Both students should be very proud."

I squeezed the back of the chair in front of me.

"Your new fifth-grade student council president is . . ."

The microphone let out a loud squeal. Mrs. Winthrop jumped back.

"Is who? Who?" I shouted, jumping up. Dumb school microphones.

Mrs. Winthrop tapped the microphone several times, but there was no sound.

She moved it out of the way and screamed, "Your new student council president is Justin Davies."

I stared at her. Everyone turned around as if looking for me.

"Justin?" Mrs. Winthrop shouted.

Carlos grabbed my arm and pulled me up. "He's here."

I stumbled past the row of kids, down the long, long aisle and up the stairs to the stage. I wished it was in slow motion. I'd won. I had really won. I hadn't even wanted to admit it to myself, but I had been worried. Andrea had put up a good battle, but this king had won the war. It was even better than I'd imagined.

I walked across the stage and listened to the whistles and cheers of the other fifth graders. Maybe there were some boos too, but it didn't matter. This was my chance to really prove that I could do this job, that someday I could be a real politician and help lots of people.

I waved at the crowd. Mrs. Winthrop held out my certificate. I grabbed the microphone instead. It still wasn't working, but my voice could carry without the sound.

I let out a long whoop, then cleared my throat. I was president now. I had to be more serious. "Thank you, everyone. I will do my best to rule . . . I mean lead, the fifth grade. This is only the beginning of my political career. And you were the first to see it happen!"

Mrs. Winthrop groaned.

I peered into the crowd until I found Andrea. I expected her to yell, "I want a recount!" Instead, she jumped up and applauded.

"I want to thank my worthy opponent, Andrea Carey, for all the good ideas she's had." I pointed to her. "We made a great team in ruling fifth grade. I promise to listen to you, and everyone."

Andrea shouted. "Hey, there's always next year's election!"

Mrs. Winthrop shoved the certificate in my hand and nudged me to the last chair on the stage. "This assembly is over. Everyone please return to your fourth-period classes in an orderly fashion."

I shook the hands of my fellow council members. Willie punched my shoulder. "Hail, Mr. President."

I punched him back.

The rest of the day was a blur. I thanked

everyone I saw, I didn't care if they voted for me or Andrea.

As soon as the last bell rang, I ran to Mrs. Winthrop's office. Andrea was already there.

"Howdy, Prez," she said.

I gave her my best presidential smile.

Mrs. Winthrop stepped out of her office. She stared at us. "Go on home, you two. Celebrate. You both did a great job."

I bowed. "Thank you. Now, let's talk about a new school sound system. I can have three or four estimates on your desk tomorrow."

Andrea stepped in front of me. "I may not be class president, but I have ideas, too. How long do you think it would take to have a tennis court built in the parking lot?"

Mrs. Winthrop backed away.

Willie ran into the office, gasping for air. "Oh, oh, Mrs. Winthrop, I'd like to discuss an idea I have for healthier lunch menus."

Mrs. Winthrop stared at the three of us. She walked into her office and slammed the door.

I shrugged. "Guess she's not ready for tennis or tofu. Don't worry, I'll come up with another great idea."

Andrea shook her head. "Not if I come up with one first."

It was going to be a wild year.